PASTURES OF TENDER GRASS

CHARLES MILLSON

GRAVE DISTRACTIONS PUBLICATIONS
NASHVILLE, TENNESSEE

PASTURES OF
TENDER GRASS

Grave Distractions Publications
Nashville, Tennessee
www.gravedistractions.com
Copyright © 2015 Charles Millson

ISBN-13: 9781944066031
In Publication Data
Millson, Charles

Primary BISAC Category: FIC026000
     FICTION / Religious
Secondary BISAC Category: FIC046000
     FICTION / Jewish

Printed in the United States

TIMELINE

THESE ARE APPROXIMATE DATES BASED ON SEVERAL SOURCES. NO HISTORICAL EVIDENCE EXISTS FOR THESE DATES.

1080 BC Saul, son of Kish, born in Benjamin.

1060 BC Jonathan is born to Saul.

1048 BC Saul is proclaimed King of Israel by Samuel, God's prophet.

1034 BC David is born to Jesse in Bethlehem of Judah

1013 BC Mephibosheth is born to Jonathan.

1008 BC Saul and Jonathan die (Jonathan in battle, Saul by his own sword).

Mephibosheth (age 5) is crippled in the escape after the battle.

1007 BC Ishbosheth declared King of Israel by Abner, captain of Saul's army.

1005 BC David made King of Israel.

997 BC David makes Jerusalem the capital of his kingdom.

996 BC David brings Mephibosheth to Jerusalem

994 BC Solomon born.

964 BC David dies; Solomon is made King of Israel.

942 BC Mephibosheth dies in Jerusalem.

CAST OF CHARACTERS

Absalom—"His father is peace" is what his name means. The son of David who kills his brother, Amnon, after Amnon rapes Absalom's full sister, Tamar. He later leads a rebellion against King David and is killed by General Joab. David married Absalom's mother to forge a peace with a neighboring kingdom.

Amnon—Original heir to David's throne. Son of Ahinoam (not Saul's wife; David's wife, from Jezreel). He rapes his sister, Tamar, causing his younger brother, Absalom, to kill him. A weak, petty, fat man who is easily swayed by his passions. His name means, "Faithful", which he was not.

Ariella—Mephibosheth's wife. The daughter of Machir and niece to Bathsheba. Thus, she is a distant relative of her husband.

Bathsheba—Sister of Machir and aunt of Mephibosheth's wife, Ariella. She becomes King David's wife after David has her husband killed in battle. Mother of King Solomon.

Ira the Jairite—Served as David's chief steward in the King's house.

Ishbosheth—As King Saul's remaining (legitimate) son, he becomes ruler of 11 of the 12 tribes of Israel for two years. He is mentally handicapped, and the real power behind his throne is his relative, Abner. He is killed by two of his generals after Abner recognizes David as king of all Israel.

Joab—David's General of the Army and his relative. Joab is, in many ways, David's hatchet man; he kills almost all of David's enemies, including David's son, Absalom. He is in turn ordered to be put to death by Solomon after David's death.

Jordana and Sheera—Servant girls of Ariella. Sheera eventually marries Ariella's son, Michah.

King David—Shepherd boy who is anointed to be Israel's next ruler by the prophet Samuel. He becomes friends with Jonathan, King Saul's son, and he becomes Saul's bitter enemy. After Saul's death, he rules Israel for about ten years in Hebron and for about thirty years in Jerusalem.

Machir—From Lo—Debar. Brother of Bathsheba and father of Ariella. Machir was a relative of Mephibosheth's mother, Sarah. One biblical source lists his father as Ammiel, the same name as listed as the father of Bathsheba.

Mephibosheth—Crippled son of Prince Jonathan and grandson of King Saul of Israel. After his father's death, he and his family live in Lo—Debar before he is brought to Jerusalem by King David to live in the King's house.

Mephibosheth (II)—Uncle of the narrator, and son of the concubine Rizpah and King Saul. He and his brother, Armoni, were given to the Gibeonites by David.

Michah—Mephibosheth's son, born in Lo—Debar, who grows to manhood in Jerusalem. He eventually has four sons of his own. He marries Sheera, the younger of his mother's servant girls.

Mordechai—Friend and servant of Mephibosheth. He had been a soldier of David's, but an injury to his arm makes him not fit for battle. He eventually manages all of Mephibosheth's ancestral lands in Benjamin.

Nathan—Prophet of God who becomes God's messenger to King David. He is given charge of the Prince Solomon and calls him Jedidiah.

Saul—Grandfather of Mephibosheth and father of Jonathan. From the tribe of Benjamin, he rules Israel for forty years. Dies in battle.

Solomon—Son of King David and second son of David's wife, Bathsheba. He is raised and taught by the prophet, Nathan, who calls him Jedidiah. Becomes King of Israel during the last days of King David's life. He is chosen by God to build the Temple in Jerusalem. Under his rule, Israel becomes wealthy and powerful.

Tamar—Sister of Ammon and Absalom (see above). She is kept in Absalom's home for years after her rape by Ammon. Absalom is her full brother. Her mother was Maacah, the daughter of King Talmai of Geshur. Absalom names a daughter after her.

Ziba—Servant who took care of Saul's traditional family lands in Benjamin. David orders him to do the same for Mephibosheth. He resents having to serve the young man, and he eventually lies to King David in order to hurt Mephibosheth and help himself.

GENEALOGY OF MEPHIBOSHETH

(* INDICATES A FICTIONAL PERSON)

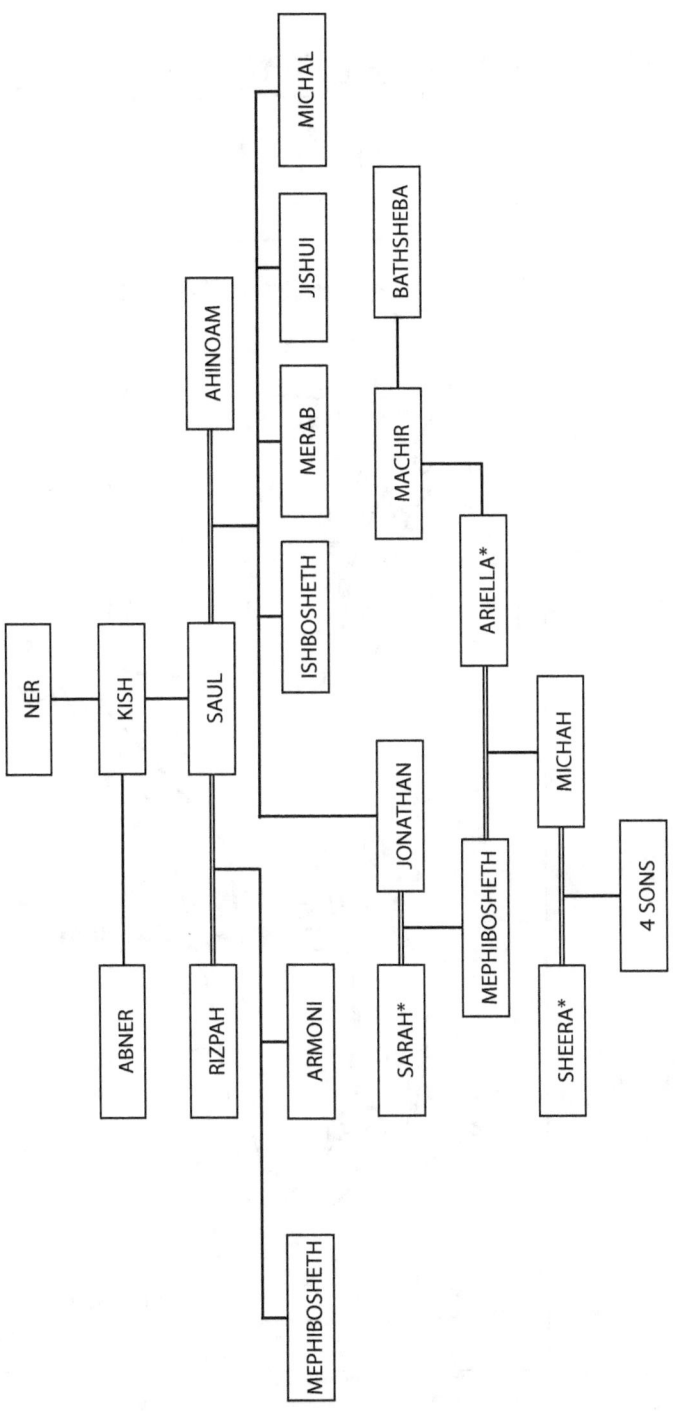

MAP OF DAVID'S AND SOLOMON'S JERUSALEM

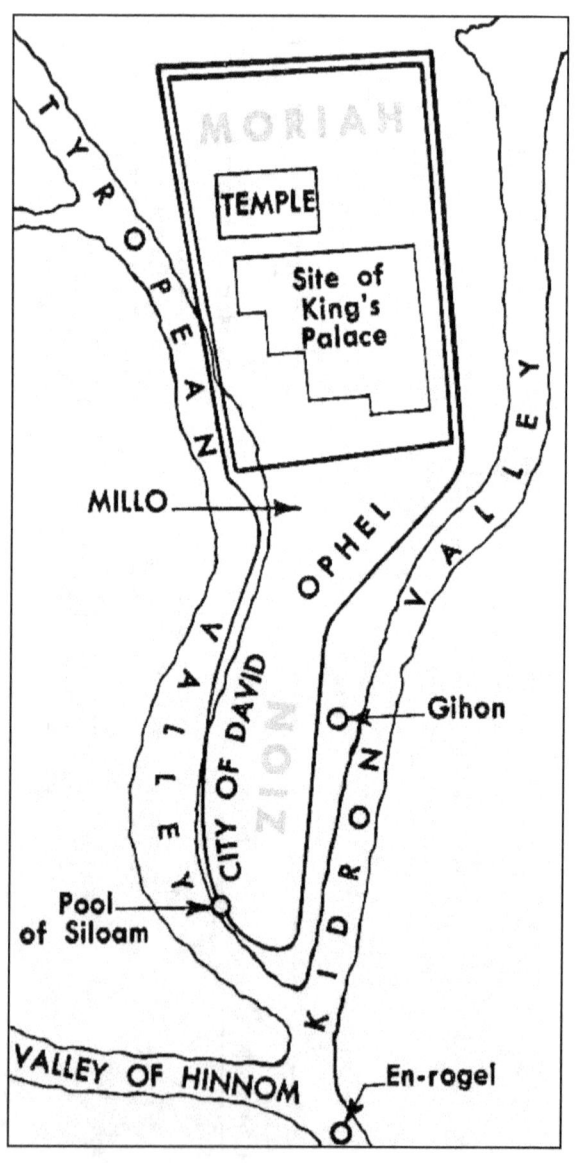

MAP OF ISRAEL IN MEPHIBOSHETH'S LIFETIME

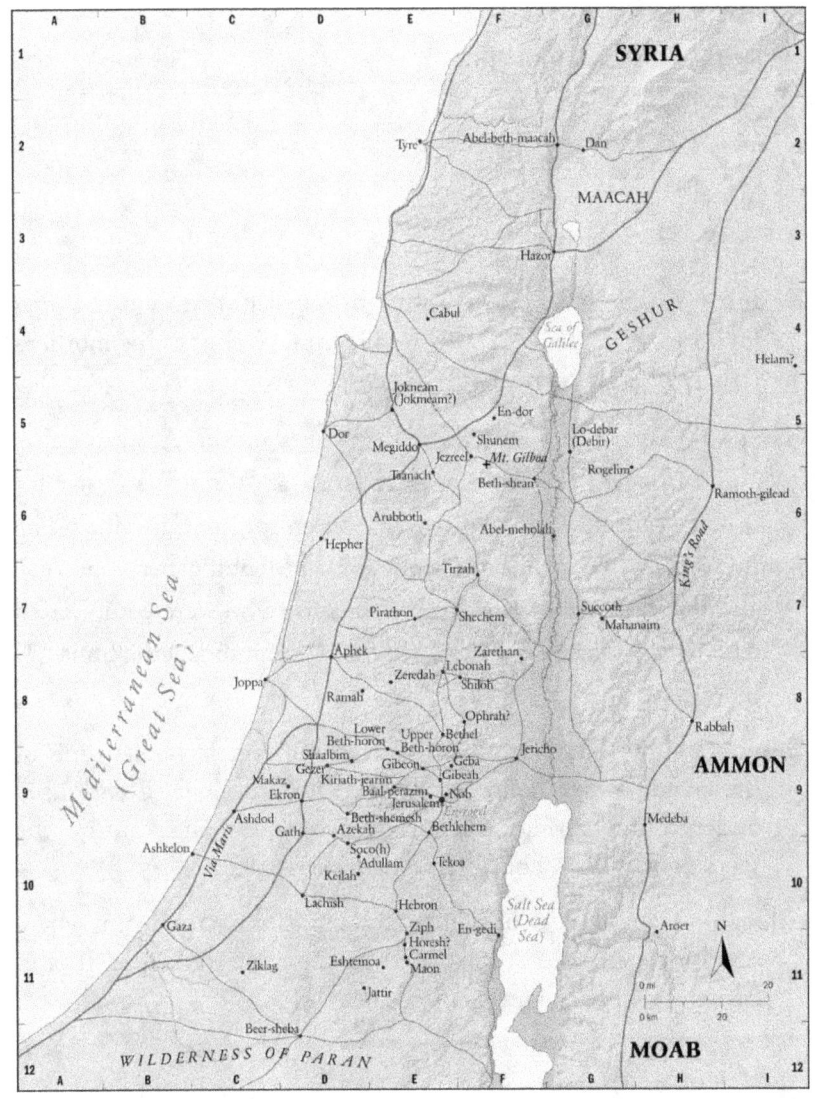

PLACE NAMES

Geshur—Absalom flees to here after the murder of Amnon and stays for three years before David recalls him. Geshur is his mother's father's city. (II Samuel 3:3)

Gibeon—City where lived the descendants of the Amorites that Saul wronged; the curse against Israel and Gibeon's desire for revenge causes David to give them "seven sons of Saul" including two sons of Rizpah, Saul's concubine (Mephibosheth's uncles), and the five sons of Merab (his cousins) who were being raised by Michal, David's (barren) wife and Mephibosheth's aunt. (II Samuel 29:1–9)

Gihon Spring—Traditional place of anointing. It is also one of the major water sources for ancient Jerusalem. David used underground springs such as this to enter and capture the seemingly impregnable fortress of Jeru—Salem.

Gilbeah—Capital city of King Saul, and the city from where Mephibosheth and Ariella tried to flee after the battle. It is in Benjamin, not too far from Jerusalem.

Hebron—David's original capital. He rules from Hebron for approximately 8 years. Most of his children are born here.

Jerusalem—The name refers to "peace"; it becomes the capital of David's nation. It is here that Mephibosheth is brought by David, and here he dies. The "City of David" occupied Mt. Zion, while what becomes the Temple mount is Mt. Moriah. David's Jerusalem is not inside the current "old city" walls.

Lo-Debar—Means "No Pasture", signifying a place of emptiness, probably land unfit even for grazing. The exact location of it is unknown, but most probably it is on the other side (i.e., east) of the Jordan River. Mephibosheth is living here with Machir, his mother's and wife's relatives, when David summons him.

Tabernacle—The Tent of Agreement constructed by Israel during the years of wandering the desert between Egypt and the Promised Land. The Ark of the Covenant was housed in the innermost court of this large tent. The Tabernacle was used by Israel as the "house of God" for almost 500 years before Solomon built the Temple in Jerusalem.

Temple—House of God built by Solomon in Jerusalem on Mt. Moriah, the traditional site where Abraham sacrifices Isaac. In David's time, it was a threshing floor. David purchased the site but God chose Solomon to build the Temple. The site lies north of and somewhat up from Mt. Zion, the area of the old City of David.

Zela—The site of the tombs of the family of Kish, the great-grandfather of Mephibosheth. David honors Saul and Jonathan and the seven descendants of Saul given as recompense to the Gibeonites by burying the family together here.

PROLOGUE

The dull clinking sound of her trowel hitting the clay jar sent a thrill down the spine of the archaeologist. She carefully pulled the trowel out of the dusty hole, laid it at her side, and reached instinctively for the camel hair paint brush she kept in the back pocket of her jeans.

The early afternoon sun above her beat down on her wide-brimmed hat, and she moved her head so the shadow of the brim would fall across place where the trowel struck the clay pot, and then she waited as the shade allowed her eyes to adjust.

The dig had been relatively successful in that artifact after artifact of been lifted from the ancient soil of the holy land. This particular dig just outside the southern walls of the old city of Jerusalem had yielded the jumbled layers of civilizations: Rock tools, shards of pottery, broken pieces of lamps, coins, and even some Roman and medieval metal.

All of it interesting. None of it earth shattering or paradigm shifting. Most of archaeology was this—the detritus of centuries of daily living in this old, old city.

Gently brushing the spot, and alternately blowing away bits of dirt, she revealed the edge of a clay pot. "Let it be intact," she prayed to herself, as she worked her way around the rim, impressed by the possibility of a large diameter jar. "An intact service bowl or large storage jar, maybe," she thought excitedly.

The rim was indeed intact, even if chipped in one place. It rested at a slight angle, sticking out of the ancient soil like a rusty-red round man buried in the sand at the beach. "Robert!" she called out to the man working on his own area not far away. "Come take a look."

As the sun made its way towards the west, the pair gently removed the dirt from around the edges of the jar, working their way slowly and insuring to support the old sides as more of the object became exposed to the air again for the first time in centuries. Periodically they would stop to photograph their progress and to exchange excited glances as they realized the increasing chances that the vessel would be intact.

The sun was low when they were finally able to remove the jar from the soil. It showed a few stress cracks but otherwise was indeed whole. The pair grinned widely at each other.

Resting and supporting the jar on the work table they could see it stood a little over a third of a meter tall. "Storage—food, maybe, but scrolls, possibly?" the woman thought. She knew it would be better to wait for the jar to be stabilized and then x-rayed to see what was inside, but she had to know—now.

Using her brush, she gently went back and forth across the opening of the jar, removing the top layer of soil.

Her heart almost stopped when a few seconds of brushwork revealed the tight coil of a scroll as it stood surrounded by all that old dirt.

ONE

Greetings to you, my dear children, from the grave. When you read this, I shall be resting with my fathers in the earth of Benjamin's tribal lands. Do not grieve for me. While my life contained much grief and pain, the blessings of Hashem, the God of all Gods, were greater by far.

Some among you who do not know my story may think I write this from a prison or one step from the sword, condemned to death by an enemy or usurper. Nothing could be more removed from the truth. I am Mephibosheth, the son of Jonathan, the son of Saul, the son of Kish of the tribe of Benjamin, and the man who should have been king of Hashem's people of Israel. I will try to tell you, the born, and you, the yet unborn, the events of my life as best as I can remember, of what I saw and heard from those who did great and terrible deeds, and try to show you, my children, how Hashem is mighty and just in His dealings with our family.

One may ask if I am bitter or angry that the crown never rested on my head. I can tell you before Hashem that I am not bitter; my conscience is clear in this matter. Being the king is neither a thing to be taken lightly, nor is it for the faint of heart. I freely confess that I am of the latter tribe. I trust that the God of Abraham, Isaac, and Jacob knew what was best for Israel when he took the crown away from my father's family, from the head of my grandfather, King Saul, and gave it to the House of David. I must be content to know that, for me, such responsibility and power was not to be, for I am not capable of such, created as I was by Hashem as an unequal among men. My dear wife Ariella (Hashem bless her name) could tell you my many faults, although out of respect she would not, if she were still alive. So, then, it falls to me to tell the story of how I came to be as I am—the undeserving yet honored guest of the present king, the Great and Wise Solomon. One may think it strange for me to be so well seen to by the family who replaced my father as heir to the throne of Israel, the man seen by many as the mortal enemy of my family.

Nor am I angry that, in my old age, I still have great pain in the dead legs I have been carrying for the past three score and six years. Again, I must trust that Hashem knew what was best for me when I became a crippled princeling. To this day, I do not remember clearly how it happened, although I have been told by several who were there and who know about the incident. I remember parts of that day well enough—mainly the panic following the defeat of my grandfather and father and the army of Israel at the great battle of Mt. Gilboa, next to the Jezreel Valley.

When we received word of the defeat and the terrible deaths of our family leaders, the entire household in Gilbeah, the king's little house (compared to the fine palace in Jerusalem in which King Solomon lives), fearing that the entire Philistine army would sweep down on us at any moment, began packing in a panic, throwing clothes and items in baskets and wagons, everyone running back and forth. I remember that the sight of adults scampering about as children brought more entertainment than panic to my five-year-old mind. So, I remember parts but not all.

What I do not recall—thank Hashem!—is the injury itself. What I have been told is that when I was snatched up and carried at the last to join the packed wagons, the nurse-girl who cared for me stumbled over the threshold of the house and sent me flying as a bird. I landed—and both of my legs crushed beneath me. I clearly remember the pain that followed. Of that I have a daily and constant reminder and will undoubtedly carry it to my grave, which will come much sooner than later. The poor girl, aged 13 at the time and a cousin of mine, carried the guilt with her for the rest of her life, despite my repeated assurances that what happened was not her doing. I told her in the intervening years that we must trust Hashem, that He knew what was best for me when I became a cripple. She would not be consoled, however, and would often weep when she looked at me.

Along with the poor remnant of our family, we escaped the Philistines and made our way to the land over the Jordan River to Lo-Debar and to the house of a distant relative, a man named Machir, the son of Ammiel. Lo-Debar is in Gilead, a mountainous area with no pastures, no green grass for grazing—a hard land in which to live and to make a living. Yet, Machir's distant relationship to my mother, Sarah, made this poor land the only—and the only safe—option remaining to what was left of most of King Saul's clan. In the remaining few years of my mother's life, she often remarked that only such poor, cursed creatures as we could come to a land so difficult. She saw it as Hashem's punishment for her father-in-law's sins. Looking at this now, I am not convinced that Hashem punished us for Saul's choices.

My mother, who was tall like my father, gave me her fine, dark hair, but she took little interest in me, so great was her grief over the events at Mt. Gilboa. Perhaps she became unwell in her mind because of her sorrow. Heartbroken at the loss of her beloved husband, Jonathan, my mother died after not too much time in Lo-Debar. (I had no idea at the time that another who loved him also deeply mourned the death of my father.) Thus, by age 10 I was lame, small, and orphaned.

At some point, my mother also had one of Machir's servants fashion some crutches for me, and I learned to get around our small house and yard with some difficulty. Yet, to me, walking with the sticks seemed to be natural after a time, despite the pain it caused me. Machir was never unkind, but I grew up around him with the impression that life there was difficult enough without having these extra mouths to feed, especially that lame one who was useless in tending to animals or the meager crops. Yet, less I appear ungrateful, before Hashem I thank Machir for his generosity in helping to raise me and allowing our desperate family to live there. He could easily have said, "No." And I am forever grateful that, when I became 15, he allowed me to marry his youngest daughter, my precious Ariella, your mother and grandmother. Of her I shall tell more.

There was also a younger sister of Machir who was around much in the early days. Sadly, my earliest memories of her are not well formed. I recall that she always smiled or laughed as she tickled me, trying to get the crippled boy to share that smile and laughter with her. Her long-lashed eyes were kind. With long, wavy brown hair that she felt no shame in showing freely, and with a long but graceful nose, she seemed to me to be a most beautiful creature. She soon married a foreigner, however, and was not around me as I grew up. To a lonely, lame boy, such a person was sorely missed, even if our time together was brief.

But I wish to tell you, dear children, of my father Jonathan, of his greatest friend King David, and of my grandfather King Saul.

TWO

King David's love for his friend, my father, was almost as strong as his love for Hashem, and certainly as strong as his ability to rule Israel. All the people know of the love that David had for Jonathan. As I said, the Prince of Israel, Jonathan, died in battle when I was five. Despite this, I have some memories of him still. He was tall, strong and handsome, with the coarse hair of that side of the family. He would throw me high up on his shoulders and laugh with me. I felt on top of the world at those moments, flying through the air as he tossed me, flying with gladness. His laugh was in contrast to his deep, resounding voice, for it was a high, almost lilting laugh that spoke of sunny days and sounded like the wind in the wheat. I am told I resemble him in the face; we share a jutting jaw and the sloping eyebrows, and his thin beard, which men in his mother's family bore, he gave to me also. However, I am like him in no other way; how could I be? I never carried a sword, never worked the fields, and never led men in any way whatsoever.

Of my grandfather, King Saul, I have no memories, and I am glad of this. He was a madman by the time I had any recognition of people and was kept from him. However, I have heard many stories of his deeds from King David, so I feel I know something about the man he was before Hashem allowed the madness to take him. Saul is where our family gets its great tallness and strength. Whether or not King Saul was a good father, I cannot say (I know my Aunt Michal hated him, but that testimony was useless, for she was a hateful, spiteful woman). To me King Saul was, and is, more like a ghost than a person. King David was always careful to tell me only the good things about my grandfather, and I appreciate his care and respect for the dead; one only had to know King David to know that he was, despite his rural upbringing, a man in whom there was no desire to speak ill of anyone—and much could have been spoken ill about King Saul. So, an accurate account of the type of man King Saul was could not be had from King David because of his kindness.

That my father was a good man is beyond question. Whatever man I became is, in part, because I wish to do no harm to his memory. He is the reason I wish to serve and honor the king. For the life of my father, at least, I am in King Saul's debt. King David told me many stories about the times before I was born, when Saul was a great warrior and my father a great soldier in his own right. As I said, I never heard King David speak of the hatred my grandfather came to have towards him; for those stories, I had to consult the records in King Solomon's archives. No, King David preferred to speak of Saul's valor and good deeds. True, King David liked to tell stories of his own exploits, but he took greater pleasure in making the tales of his friends always seem greater than his own triumphs, and he loved to give credit to Hashem and to all those who helped him in battle. Such a man was King David.

When he was but a shepherd boy (who has not heard this story? It is to this day still told to the young as an example of what any person in Israel can do with the strength of Hashem!), King David fought the great giant warrior of the Philistines, Goliath from Gath, and killed him with his sling and one stone. The ruddy, rough boy with red hair from Bethlehem, the sweet smell of lamb's milk still on his skin, came to King Saul's army camp as the Israelites faced the Philistine army to bring some food from home to his older brothers. He heard the taunting of the giant from Gath, and he was amazed that no one in Saul's army would answer the uncircumcised idolater. King David liked to say that it was my father who advised him to aim his sling at the forehead of the Philistine. I do not know for sure whether this is true since, as I have said, King David liked to put his friends in his stories. It does not matter. What does matter, and is beyond dispute, is that soon after great Goliath's head lay separated from his shoulders, the shepherd boy David was taken into the household of my grandfather to be his armor bearer, and he then became the constant companion of the Crown Prince Jonathan.

King David was also a man of the fields, like my grandfather the King. Despite the enmity Saul came to feel for David, I am certain they had much more in common than either of them would have with the present King. King Solomon's hands, like my own, betray the fact that he has never carried a sword or steadied a plow or worked a day in his life. Yet, he has great wisdom, and the world knows it. And he has been extraordinarily kind to me and to our family, as was his father before him.

I have always thought it odd that my grandfather were to be the chosen one by Hashem through the prophet and judge, Samuel. As I have said, we came from Benjamin, the smallest tribe, and you already know that ours is the smallest family of that tribe. Saul, like all of our family, was a shepherd. The madness that took him in his later life was said to have been present in our family for several generations. After his suicide during the battle near the Valley of Jezreel, Saul's ultimately disappointing reign and life were enough to cause the women in our family to make a sign of luck whenever his name was spoken—which was rarely in our house. I do not hold to these superstitions, but one does not speak lightly of the dead; it does not matter how they lived or died. Yet, King David told me that Saul once had the gift of prophecy, which Hashem also does not dispense lightly. The wise men always say that it is a short journey from prophet to madman, and perhaps this was the case with my grandfather. I believe that the choice of Saul as king was Hashem's way of telling Israel that even—and maybe especially—the weakest among us can do anything with His help. Again, all of that was long before the madness took him which led to his death and, incidentally, my crippling.

My grandmother was the favorite of King Saul's two wives. Her name was Ahinoam and, like her name suggests, she was a kind woman. The daughter of Ahimaaz, a man who owned large areas of land in Benjamin, she had the short stature of her father. She took charge of my raising after my mother's death. In her kindness, she told me as a boy that my shortness came from her side of the family (I knew my short stature came from my crippled legs, but for a child to hear this makes him feel better, and I am grateful to her). I have many stories of her, for she lived to see my son Michah, and she outlived all her sons, which should not be. She also had more children by Saul than did his other wife and his two concubines combined so, in her mind, Hashem blessed her despite her manifold heartaches. Even in her old age, when wars and retributions had wiped out most of her family, she still gave praise to the God of Israel, thanking Him for her children and for her long life.

My father Jonathan was her eldest and her favorite. How the same family could produce a Jonathan and a Michal is beyond my understanding, but there it is. So, yes, Jonathan was the beloved of my grandmother. There was a special love between them—I saw it in her eyes when she spoke of him. He seemed to inspire such in all he met. Jonathan grew up at her side until he was of an age to help his father in the fields. Even after he left her to take his place among the men, she said Jonathan never forgot her. He would bring her small presents on special occasions or none, and he would see to it that she had the things she needed and many she did not need. According to King David, it was Jonathan who suggested that King Saul set up a chair for Ahinoam in the Audience Room at the small house in Gilbeah out of respect for her position as the mother of the next king. This was never done by Saul, but King Solomon has set up such a place in his Audience Room for his mother, the great beauty Bathsheba. It is possible that my father wished to honor his mother in such a way, so great was his respect for her—as any son should respect his mother. Yet, it was not done until Solomon's time.

Even as a young man, my father accomplished feats that foretold greatness. Early in the reign of Saul, he and his servant boy won a great victory. King David repeated the story often around the modest wooden dinner table in his house (I say modest because the house it was in was but a large country house compared to Solomon's Palace). In the tale, Jonathan and his servant boy scaled a great cliff wall and surprised the enemy and routed them—only the two of them! David told this story as if he were the servant boy, although he never stated this as a fact. He told the story to show that even two men and Hashem can defeat an army. Jonathan even killed two dozen Philistines by himself and set the enemy to rout at the battle of Micmash while his father was back at his camp trying to decide on a strategy.

Yes, Jonathan would have been a great king for Hashem and for Israel. Unlike Saul, Jonathan learned to hold a writing tool and to read more of the Law than many priests of Israel. I hold dear a memory of him reading a tablet at a small table beside a lamp. Perhaps this image served as an inspiration to me to want to learn as much as I could. Besides, with such boyish pursuits as running and jumping and fighting beyond the limits of my legs, I found in reading and writing a way to, in part, make up for my weak legs. And, truth be told, it seemed a way for me to be more like the father I never got to know and still miss.

By the time my father joined his father in battle, near the age of 20, Israel had changed from a loose gathering of tribes to a people who were united under Saul's leadership. Saul's great victory over Hashem's foes at Jabesh Gilead told the people that they had found a champion and a fighter, and they followed him. The army of farmers with crude wooden weapons which had followed Saul into battle was soon transformed into a small but effective permanent standing army, with metal weapons, ready to go to war with any enemy. The tribes of Israel could even supply more men if needed, but Saul kept a group of men around him permanently. That brave but small band is in contrast to the large, well-trained and equipped might of Solomon's army. It causes one to laugh to think of the army of Saul facing King Solomon's forces. Today's army of Israel ranks among the world's best: Sharp-edged war chariots, Cavalry, spearmen, armored archers—all with the best weapons and supplies—the best of the best for King Solomon. Odd, really, since King Solomon has had little use for his army, unlike the almost constant warfare that Saul and then David had to face for so long.

But I digress. Still, the contrast is great in this and in most of the other things I have seen in my lifetime. Forgive me, dear children, if the ramblings of an old man become confused and scattered. I wish to think of it all for your benefit. Where was I? Oh, yes; my father.

Not only did King David admit it, but also King Solomon does as well: Jonathan would have been a great king of Israel. If only Saul had shared his son's belief that Hashem was greater than anything else! But as I said, I am not bitter. Once King David, in a moment when few others were around, told me in a loud voice (he grew hard of hearing as an old man and often spoke louder than he intended) that when Jonathan died and he wept over his death, he was also weeping for Israel. It was the way King David had of involving the listener in what he was saying. David wanted me to ask the question to which he had led me, so I asked, "Why did you weep for Israel?" "I wept," he said, his tired eyes glistening with tears still, "because Jonathan was the great King of Israel that Israel would never have and under whose rule would have prospered." That moment was yet another great gift from King David that I shall cherish until I die.

THREE

The person about whom I have spoken little so far in this retelling, my children, is the prophet Samuel. His origins remain shrouded in the amazing: His birth was miraculous, his upbringing was unusual, and his life as Hashem's prophet and judge astonishing. My grandmother would say only that he was a man of Hashem and leave it at that. My Aunt Michal, who intrigued and gossiped, liked to tell me the story that he was something else. She swore that Samuel practiced more than the rituals assigned to Hashem, that he was a diviner of the type that King Solomon keeps in court to entertain us nowadays, a conjurer. My Aunt Michal swore that Samuel put a curse on my grandfather and on our family. About this I do not know; her testimony is questionable at best because she was, as I have said, a bitter woman.

What I do know is that it was after the battle of Micmash, and after a visit from the prophet Samuel, that King Saul began showing signs of the sickness in his head that would lead to everything that has happened to our family. Samuel came to Saul to tell him that the King had been impatient and should have trusted Hashem and that, because of his lack of trust, Hashem's trust in Saul had been removed, along with the crown. I have spoken with several people regarding this matter, and they all confirm that these events took place. Hashem's will be done. The scribes with whom I now work in Solomon's archives and who keep the official records (David started this practice, not Saul or Solomon) tell me that the history of Saul that is the official one indicates that this is the point in the story of our family where David enters the narrative, but I have my doubts about that. The scroll to which they refer records that Saul began having terrible aches in his head after Samuel's visit and that David was summoned from his shepherding fields to play his music for King Saul and to soothe his pain.

As I sit now in my rooms of King Solomon's Palace, with an expansive view of the city of Jerusalem, it is difficult to imagine that all I see before me was created in less than 100 years. If one were to see the land before all this, he would be surprised to learn that Israel was indeed a scattering of villages and farms. I know this to be true because that is where Samuel found Saul when Hashem chose my grandfather to be Israel's first king. King Solomon, who never goes anywhere without a large group of servants, would find it impossible and unthinkable to go, as Handsome Saul (as he was known) did, after some runaway donkeys with only one servant, much less chase some runaway donkeys! But it was on this search that Saul encountered Samuel, and Samuel announced that Saul was the Chosen One of Hashem to lead Israel as king. It was there that Samuel anointed my grandfather with olive oil and kissed him and blessed him.

This encounter stands in sharp contrast with the last time the two met years afterward. Saul, in his madness and desperation, and nearing his end, secretly attempted to contact the then-dead Samuel through a seer. Samuel's image, according to the story, appeared and told my grandfather, "Why do you bother me—Hashem has left you and is now your enemy. David will now be king. You and your sons will die tomorrow in battle." Two men accompanied my grandfather to this seer, and this story I heard from one of them many years later.

Thus, Samuel remains one of the most important people in the history of our family, even though no one is left alive today who knew him.

I must stop at this point, my children. Consider this: I, and therefore you, know more about our family's story from others and from the man who replaced King Saul than we know from our own family. It still amazes me to think of it. It remains a testimony to the goodness of King David and his family; never forget that. Still, King David's version of the story is slightly different. I suspect that the account in the archives that lies bound and sealed comes from the mind of our King Solomon and, as king, that is his prerogative. And who can begrudge the king?

Thus, to make the record clear regarding our family, Samuel's prophecy concerning our family was from Hashem and it was true: My father and grandfather were indeed killed in battle the next day, and another family eventually became the kings of Israel. Even the spirit of Samuel prophesied because of Hashem's power. And it was at Lo-Debar that I grew into young manhood, hearing bits and pieces of this story, learning all I could from my grandmother and others in our family, marrying Ariella, and eventually having a son of my own, Michah. And perhaps you can understand that I grew to be a fearful, timid, and quiet young man who struggled to understand what had happened to our family. Despite this, and largely because of my grandmother, I soon learned early, and how, even in despair and in Lo-Debar, Hashem can be merciful.

Meanwhile, without our knowledge, and several miles away, a former servant of my grandfather re-entered the story and changed our lives forever.

FOUR

While we watched from afar in Lo-Debar, Israel struggled. The deaths of Saul and Jonathan left the people without a true leader. David was not yet in a position to become the leader Israel needed and wanted, but soon he would be. Until then, the next in line to Saul's throne was my idiot uncle who was, sadly, not at all like my grandfather or father—a "man" named Ishbosheth. The madness that afflicted my grandfather manifested itself differently in my uncle. His head never grew as his body did, and it was as if he were always five years old. He was controlled by a great uncle of mine, Abner, who was a general in Saul's army and at one time a mighty man of valor. Abner, seeing that no king was left, propped up Ishbosheth as a true king with himself as the power behind the child.

Yes, Abner indeed passed off this pretend king for most of Israel, but Judah, the most powerful tribe, refused to recognize him—the men of Judah were waiting for David to arrive as king. Judah's men were wise because they knew of Hashem's prophecy and, besides, there were no other real options. For two years, Ishbosheth played with toys and had to have help getting to sleep at night, while Abner tried to find a way to increase his power. Meanwhile, Israel suffered the uncertainty of poor leadership. A short war between the two factions—Abner/Ishbosheth against David—resulted in Abner siding with David when he realized that his position was untenable. Abner's reversal of loyalty was a death sentence to my poor, slow-witted uncle, who was killed by two of his generals as he took his afternoon nap. Perhaps there was mercy in that. He was quickly buried and mourned by no one.

The death of Ishbosheth opened the door for David to be proclaimed king of the whole of Israel. While more bloodshed followed in the consolidation of power, David soon united the people. He then moved to take the hill fortress of Jerusalem and made it his capital city. All of this we heard in bits and pieces since we were so far removed from the intrigue and action. The details, of course, I heard much later, and from many of those who were involved in the events. Still, the news of the ascension of David caused no little fear among the family, since Israel had never before seen a change in the family line of the king. Something of a panic swept through the women as they spoke of the possibility of David wiping out the line of potential usurpers or rivals. They knew that I was one such. It is what a king does when there are potential claimants to the throne. This I know because I have witnessed it myself in the years since. At the time, it was even whispered that Machir was starting to have second thoughts about harboring our little brood. He spoke loudly about his loyalty to David, even if he were distantly related to us and hosted us in our exile.

It was at this point, in my seventeenth year, that messengers arrived from King David with the news we feared the most: I was being summoned by the new king to his new capital, Jerusalem. My children, I cannot tell you the fear with which I received this news.

I remember the moment clearly. Ariella was holding Michah and we were sitting outside of the little house that Machir had given us next to his larger dwelling. I was trying to teach Ariella how to read—she had a quick mind, but never saw the use of reading and, besides, she now had a son to care for as well as a lame husband. We were laughing about some trifle when two riders approached with another, riderless mule. One of the men was older than the other, but they resembled each other, so it seemed clear that they were father and son. As they pulled up in front of our dwelling, Ariella grabbed Michah and took him inside. "Is this the house of Mephibosheth, the son of Jonathan, the son of Saul?" the older one asked. He looked at my legs and nodded, as if the twisted limbs confirmed his question. "Yes," I said, "I am Mephibosheth. Please forgive me if I don't stand." Both men were tall, and their attitudes were brusque. I called to Ariella to bring them some water and food as they dismounted.

Word had spread in Lo-Debar that the men were looking for me. My grandmother, breathless from running from her nearby house, was close on their heels, followed by other women in our family. The men stood over me, their faces blocking out the light and not letting me see their expressions or features. I could tell, however, even as they blocked the light, that their clothes were finer than what I was used to.

"Ziba? Ziba, the son of Isaac? Is that you?" my grandmother gasped when she got close enough. The men turned to face her.

"Yes," the older man said, "It is I. Greetings, Ahinoam, wife of Saul."

As he turned, I could see that there were great gaps where teeth had once been and that his beard grew to a sharp point below his chin, much like a goat's beard. My grandmother ran up to him as if to grab him, but she pulled back and asked, still out of breath,

"What do you want of him? What do you want with my son?"

"Your grandson," the younger man rudely corrected her.

The older man ignored them both and turned back to me.

"I am Ziba, the servant of King David of Israel. The King has ordered me to bring you to him immediately."

My grandmother and the other women fell to their knees and wailed. Ariella came out with a pitcher of water and some bread, but she stood at the table holding them instead of setting them down. She had heard what the older man had said, and she had heard the wails of the other women. She told me later that she was shocked into stillness, and that's why she showed no emotion. From inside the house, I heard Michah starting to fret that his mother was not holding him, and perhaps he also had heard the wailing from outside.

Many times in my short life, until that point, I had wondered why I had been spared the death that had taken almost all the other men of my family. Much of my early life was spent in fear of the sword, from Abner or from another who wished to stamp out any possible pretender to the throne. As we heard of the rise of David, some in the family surmised that he would take steps to ensure that no one, at least from Saul's family, could assert a claim. After all, how many injuries had Saul attempted on David? How many times did David have to hide in fear of his life from my grandfather? It seemed that Hashem, in His wisdom, had decided that this was the time for vengeance. Over the years, I knew that many of the prayers of my wife and my grandmother and others included appeals to Hashem to spare me from the sword at David's hand and anger. With great passion, they pleaded for Hashem to not seek retribution on my head for the sins of Saul. And now it seemed as if Hashem had not heard those prayers.

The men waited as if seeing what my response to this summons would be. Flight was, obviously, impossible. Even if David had sent a child to take me, I could not have defended myself. There was nothing else to do except submit to Hashem's will. With that thought, and wanting these men to say that I went to my death bravely in honor of my father, I came to my senses and returned to a sense of calm at the thought of him. I know my voice shook, but I managed to say to them,

"Won't you sit a moment and have some water? You must be thirsty."

FIVE

Much of the rest of that day is difficult to remember. Someone must have gone to find Machir, because he soon arrived. To my surprise, even Machir began to plead with the men to not take me to David, that I was a lame young man—a bit touched even, because I liked only learning, touched as his grandfather was, Machir said—and was a threat to no one. Perhaps, he thought, even a lame son-in-law was better than a dead one. Perhaps he did not want to have to care for an infant grandson. Meanwhile, my grandmother continued her pleas as did many of the other family members. The men—Ziba the father and, as it turned out, his oldest son Reuben—listened impassively to all the supplications of Machir and my grandmother. They did accept the water and bread Ariella offered after I called her attention to the fact that she still had yet to set the items on the table. "We have our orders," was all that Ziba seemed to say. And somewhere during the next hour or so I learned exactly who Ziba was, although I can't exactly remember from whom I learned that.

Ziba had been my grandfather's chief servant. He ran not only the house at Gilbeah, but he also was the superintendent of the lands of the king—the farms and forests—and looked over all his livestock as well. More than a servant, his real role was that of making sure that the king's possessions were profitable and protected. That seemed to satisfy my mind at the time as to why he did not join us in exile in Lo-Debar. Not until later did I find out that, upon Saul's death and the chaos that followed, Ziba had quietly continued to perform his duties rather admirably. In fact, he caused the lands and farms to prosper quite well. He and his fifteen sons and a coterie of servants continued to collect taxes, make repairs, and take care of the servant workers on the land. In this, I cannot fault him. He did his job. However, the reason Ziba performed his duties as admirably as he did was not out of loyalty to Saul or as one should because Hashem deserves our best before Him. No, Ziba took care of the land because, in the absence of his lord or any claimant, he saw that he himself had become the owner and lord of the land by default. I accuse him of this because I know it to be true, my children. One does not disparage out of ignorance, ever. And now, as he sat with his goat-beard and his serious and rude son at the little rough table outside my small house, surrounded by my pleading relatives, I am confident that Ziba felt put out and not a little bit angered. After all, he had to leave the comfort of "his" lands in order to run an errand for King David to find this silly, crippled, useless young man who might make trouble for him and possibly claim the lands he and his family had worked so hard and so well to improve.

Although none of us knew it at the time, Ziba's task was actually one of great joy on the king's part. After he had consolidated his power, and after he had secured Jerusalem and made it the capital city of Israel, King David had time to repay what he felt was an old debt to his departed best friend, my father. He kept his word, as was David's wont. In much later years, I came to believe that the loss of Jonathan hurt King David more than almost any loss he suffered in his lifetime—and there were many, many terrible losses. But, as all know, his love for my father was great. The consolidation of his power as king had not been too difficult for David. The rocky outcrop fortress of Jerusalem remained a holdout, that village that was one of the oldest in the land because of its prime position as the highest point for some distance. It was thought to have been impregnable. David solved it, however, by using the ancient water supply system under the rock to bring his men inside. The capture of the Jerusalem fortress meant that David could take stock of his position for the first time; it allowed him to catch his breath. He was secure in power and he had his capital. It was the moment now to keep his promises to an old friend and before Hashem.

"Is there anyone left from Saul's family?" King David asked one day as he and his court sat at the dining table of his house. Looking down the rows of faces on each side of that table, faces that turned to each other with questioning looks, David repeated his question.

"Come, come; is there anyone left of Saul's family?"

The answer, aside from the shrugged shoulders of everyone else, came from the king's chief steward, a man I would come to know well, one Ira the Jairite. "My King!" Ira said, as he leaned the wine pitcher over King David's shoulder. "Someone who might know is King Saul's chief servant, Ziba. He is the head of the lands of Saul in Benjamin. Perhaps you could send for him and inquire?"

Two or three men leaped to volunteer. Ziba was summoned, and he appeared before David two days later.

"Oh, great King David!" Ziba said, prostrating himself in front of the throne in the Audience Room of the king's house. "How can your servant be of help?"

"Tell me of Saul's remaining family, Ziba. You may rise."

Ziba rose and straightened himself. He paused—perhaps too long for King David's liking.

"Well?" King David asked, "Tell me. Is there any remnant of Jonathan, the son of Saul?"

"Ah, of Jonathan," Ziba repeated, seeming to buy himself some time for the answer he felt the King wanted. "Yes. There is a son who survived after the defeat of King Saul and the death of Prince Jonathan at Mt. Gilboa." At this news, David leaned forward in his chair, worry lining his brow. Ziba continued,

"Ah, but do not worry yourself, King David! He is lame and will be of no trouble to you. He lives with a relative across the Jordan, in a poor place called Lo-Debar."

A great gladness broke over the king's face. "He doesn't worry me, Ziba; I don't want to harm him," King David answered.

Ziba looked at the King with puzzlement. "Then, what can I do for you, my King?" he asked.

"I want you to retrieve this son of Jonathan," David continued. "I want to honor him."

Ziba's goat-face sagged visibly, his jaw becoming slack in amazement. Perhaps such a thought of honoring someone else or of keeping true trust before Hashem was foreign to one such as he was. Instead of eliminating any claimant to what he had, as Ziba no doubt would have done, David instead wished to bestow a blessing.

All of this I learned much later from Ira the Jairite himself. The king dispatched three mules and Ziba and Ziba's son to fetch me and bring me back to Jerusalem. He even gave Ziba gifts to bring to me to show me that he meant me no harm. So Ziba set out on a journey he did not want to make to get a lame prince who could only hurt his plan to control the lands and property of his former master, King Saul. Perhaps it was on this journey that he made his plans to harm me and my family even more than we had been harmed.

Who knows the heart of man except Hashem?

SIX

I do know that the gifts were not presented when Ziba and his son arrived. Nor were they presented when, my eyes filling with tears despite my resolve to be brave in my father's memory, I was carried and placed on the mule that Ziba led. Instead of honoring me as David intended, Ziba decided to torture me by treating me like the prisoner I thought I was about to become. The gifts were also not left with my still-stunned wife and crying grandmother and screaming son and distraught family, all of whom, as I left their sight, thought they were never to see me again, nor I them. Before we set out, Ziba did not even allow me to change my clothes from the simple garment that I wore around the house. At the last, however, he reluctantly let Machir place my crutches on the side of my mule, but that was his only concession. Otherwise, nothing else was granted me—not my tablets or any other reminder of the life I had known. From my perch on the mule being led away, I could not turn to see my beloved family as they wept with anguish at my departure. My children, I tell you this: To this day, all these decades later, the thought of all that pain in the hearts of my loved ones hurts me.

Ziba did not make the journey easier. He refused to stop to allow me to relieve myself, and he would only allow me water when he had some. Such was his pettiness and evil heart. He and Reuben spoke to each other little, in whispered tones I could not make out, and neither one spoke to me much at all. No, Ziba said little during the two-day journey to Jerusalem. His son took care of the mules during the stops we made, and we found lodging in two villages along the way. Ziba made sure that the charge for the room was made to King David. I had never spent a night away from my family. Even at age 17, such a new thing would be hard for anyone who was unused to it. I confess to stifling cries into the blanket given me. I missed my little house and my son and my Ariella. Besides, Ziba and his son snored worse than anyone I had ever heard, and they produced gas so loud and noxious—all of which added to my fears about meeting the king and made my two nights on the journey mostly sleepless ones.

Such was Ziba's cruelty that he never spoke of King David's intentions towards me until the night before we were to reach Jerusalem. I then saw, because he showed me, the gifts that the king had given him and that had been stashed on his and his son's mules— gold, spices, incense—gifts that my family could surely use and had needed for some time. Living off the generosity of relatives, not being able to provide for one's family—those things eat at a man, whether he has good legs or none. Ziba said that David gave them "for you," but I did not exactly understand what he meant. Perhaps these gifts really were not meant for me; perhaps they were Ziba's payment for bringing me back to King David.

It was that last morning before we reached the city that Ziba threw clothes in my face with the order to, "Put these on." They were the nicest clothes I had ever owned, but they were much too large and therefore terribly ill-fitting. The man then tried (and succeeded) to scare me with what King David wanted from me. He said that the king wished to speak to me about my father, but he never explained that King David wished to remember his oath to Jonathan, the oath to care for each other's families, by bringing me to live with him. What little sleep I received the night before we arrived was blessed by a vision of my father as I remembered him, laughing with me and tossing me on his shoulder. This comforted me somewhat, and I honor Hashem for sending it to me. As we came up and down the hills and valleys towards Jerusalem, I grew anxious. What would the king say? The gifts, if they were meant for me, indicated that King David planned me no harm, perhaps, but I had learned to wait to see the truth for myself.

The idea that the shepherd fortress of Jeru-Salem would become the beautiful capital city of a great nation, known and admired throughout the world, would have been absurd to my grandfather. The rustic market town that Saul had chosen as his capital seat, Gilbeah, will never see the rainbow of humanity that now daily parades through Solomon's Jerusalem, its black-bricked streets bustling with activity, filled with different cultures and religions, diplomats, merchants, traders, caravans, courtiers, the royal family, and the simply curious. All intermingle in a truly international city, as tongues found everywhere from the banks of the Tigris to the flooded fields of the Nile, and even beyond these, can be heard here today. At the time I first entered Jerusalem, being led like a woman behind Ziba, the city was still very much a town. David had only started his rebuilding of the citadel and the fortifying of the walls. No true palace had been built and, certainly, no glorious Temple of Hashem had been erected. It does indeed seem like more than two generations removed. It seems like two thousand. From stock herders to being the host of the Queen of Sheba in two generations would be laughable if it were not true, and all this I have seen with my own eyes, which are not as crippled as my legs, although they are old.

It was thus that Ziba brought me into the presence of King David of Israel, the man who had taken the throne of my grandfather.

SEVEN

A s I have said, compared to Solomon's palace, the house that David lived in at that time was modest. However, to a young man such as I, a man who had seen almost nothing of the world and having little memory of my grandfather's house in Gilbeah, it seemed to me to be the grandest house imaginable. I heard the whispers from those outside, servants and soldiers alike, as I was assisted to the ground in front of the house and handed my sticks from the side of the mule. I felt their eyes as Ziba walked briskly ahead of me, stopping impatiently every so often while I caught up with him the best I could by using my crutches. The clothes given me did not help my progress. Though finer than any I had ever owned, they were, as I have said, made for someone larger. My crippled legs and my crutches kept getting snagged on the hem of the garment. Through the long hallway to the king's dining room, my nervousness increased. Surely, if he had meant to kill me, he could have easily dispatched me in Lo-Debar and have been done with it. So, I reasoned, surely he would not put me to the sword, at least not immediately. But then, if not that, what? It is the not knowing that always makes it worse.

Suddenly, the doors ahead of us were opened by two large armed men, and there stood King David. While I saw that many people were behind him, I couldn't take my eyes off him. Tall, handsome, with darker skin than most men, but reddish hair with some spaces of gray beginning to show, a full set of teeth—in short, a man in the prime of his life and powers. David, as I first saw him, was dressed not as a king in a great robe as his son King Solomon wears now, but rather in a soldier's shorter, simpler robe with rough threaded details worked into fringe. Fine, flowing clothing never suited King David. Across his face was an expansive smile—but I could not tell if it were a smile of triumph, joy, or satisfaction. Simply being in his presence at last caused me to drop my crutches and fall to my knees in the doorway, ignoring the pain.

The King's smile abruptly ended, and he looked shocked at my actions. The first words King David said to me were,

"Are you Mephibosheth?" "Yes, I am, Your Majesty."

King David said, "Don't be afraid, young man," almost as an order. It did not lessen my fear. Turning to another, shorter bald man, he said, "Ira, assist him. Help him stand."

The round-faced bald man and another servant quickly came to me and lifted me off my knees with little effort since I was and am, as you know, quite small. As I looked back up at the king, he was now smiling again, but great tears were running down his cheeks.

"By Hashem! You look like your father!" David exclaimed when the two men carrying me swung me around to face him. "Get him a chair," he ordered. "Get one for me, too."

The crowd behind him tittered. I think they could not believe that David would bring me, a crying, weak cripple in oversized clothes, and the grandson of his greatest enemy, into his house and treat me as a guest. Especially someone who was a potential heir to the throne he occupied. As for me, I was beyond speechless as this activity commenced. Next, on orders from the king, another servant produced a ewer of warm water and washed my feet and legs, taking care not to turn them too much when I tensed with pain. The King also asked that some water for me to drink be brought. I took it with thanks. Somewhere in all this movement, I saw Ziba standing to the side, his eyes burning with both curiosity and disdain.

Meanwhile, King David continued to talk to me as if we had known each other for some time. I am sure his first impression of me was that I was an idiot in the order of my uncle Ishbosheth because I barely answered him and, when I did, the answers were usually short ones.

"Did you have trouble on the journey?"

"No, my king." It was the first untruth I ever told anyone.

"Do your legs hurt you much? I mean, do they trouble you much?"

"Yes, sir."

He showed concern on his face, and he reminded the servant to take care in washing my dead legs.

"How is your mother?"

"Dead, sire."

"Hmm... Sorry to hear that. She was a good woman."

"Yes, sire."

His tears had dried up as the questions continued. He seemed genuinely interested in learning about me.

"Do you have memories of your father?"

"Few, sir," I answered. What was the King doing? Why the questioning?

"Do you have a family?"

"A wife and a son, my lord."

"A son! A wife! Praise Hashem!" He shouted loudly, scaring me somewhat. He moved forward in his chair, his knees spread wide as he slapped one of them.

"Yes!" I said, suddenly agreeing with King David, "Praise Him!"

"Did your family like the presents I sent by Ziba?"

Here I hesitated and saw, out of the corner of my eye, that Ziba became startled. Part of me said to tell the king that I had not even seen the presents until the night before, that Ziba had withheld them from my family. However, I did not know yet for certain whom I could trust in this new place, and thought it wiser to hold back.

"I… I…" The right words suddenly came to me. "Your servant is undeserving of gifts," I said finally. Ziba let out a held breath.

David considered this. "We shall see." He turned to Ira and nodded. The bald man handed the King something from a closed fist.

"Mephibosheth, I made a promise to your father many years ago—the same promise he made to me. Here is what we said to each other. If something happened to me, he would take care of my family. If something happened to him, I would take care of his family."

There. It was for this that he had brought me to Jerusalem. Not punishment, not imprisonment, not torture, not death. Mercy.

"I will be kind to you because of your father. If he were where I am, and I where he is, he would do the same for my family. Do you understand?"

I nodded in disbelief. I did not truly understand. A second lie.

"I'm going to start by bringing your wife—what is her name?— and your son here to live with you in my house. Then, I'm going to give you back the land that belonged to your grandfather Saul."

Ziba's mouth flew open, but I was the only one who noticed because everyone else's mouths were already ajar. I'm sure my own mouth was agape as well. What David was saying was unprecedented. Who had ever heard of such generosity to the son of a rival, the grandson of the man who had tried so many times to kill the giver of these things? Yet, King David was not through.

"Besides that, you will always eat with me at my table. I have always wanted to see Jonathan's face at my table and, having you there, I always shall."

Suddenly, it was all too much. I could not restrain my emotion. I thrashed violently out of the chair, knocking over the ewer and sending the servant sprawling. The crowd gasped loudly, and I think a woman among them screamed something. With my face to the floor in the puddle of water, I could only cry through my tears, "Why should you care about me? I'm worth no more than a dead dog."

David was crying, too. He, the great king of Israel, knelt beside me and helped me back into the chair, soothing me by patting my head, as if I were a scared lamb in his flock, which, at that moment, I was. "Hush, now, you're tired. It will all be well. You are worthy to me, if for no other reason than that you are the son of the greatest man I ever knew."

When he had me seated again, he took my hand and held it before both of us. His palms felt rough and large around my smaller, softer hand. From his closed fist he took a ring, the object the bald man had handed him. The King placed it on my finger. It was gold with a lapis stone set in it.

"This is the sign of my covenant with you and your father," David explained. "Wear this ring to remember that I will keep my word to you before Hashem because of your father, Jonathan."

I loved King David from that moment on. It was also now much easier for me to understand my father and how he felt about the king—such a heart as his is easy to love. That, too, was a gift that King David gave me, my children. It is why, as the poets have said, King David even captured the heart of Hashem with his love.

"Dry your tears, my son." ("My son!" he called me, and I remember thinking, "How wonderful! No man had ever called me that before to my memory.") "We will have much time to discuss many more things later. You need to get cleaned up from your journey and rested."

He touched my arm affectionately and finally noticed that my clothes were outsized. "No, no; this won't do. My apologies, Mephibosheth. We will make better fitting clothes for you. I didn't know your size. It is all my fault." The King, apologizing to me! If blood could have come out of Ziba's ears at that moment, I am certain it would have.

"Here," he said, pulling up the garment under my arms, "and here," he added, gathering the cloth above the knees. "That will do until we can get new ones later. Ira, will you see to it, please?"

"Of course, my King," Ira answered.

"Your servant thanks you, my King," I said.

"Ah, he has manners about him. What do you think about that, Ira?" David said, smilingly, turning to the chief steward. "He might teach us a thing or two about how to act around this barracks of a house, what do you think?""

As you say, my King," Ira answered again.

"Look!" he said, pointing behind us, "There is your Aunt Michal! You know who she is, surely! She is my wife. I am your uncle, Mephibosheth!" David laughed, turning and holding out his hand to a tall, thin woman with a weak chin who stepped out of the crowd behind him. Yes, it was obvious that she was my father's sister, the height and dark hair and strong eyes gave that away, but there was no kindness behind these features. I had never met her before that I remembered, but I knew of her, and said so. She looked at me through a squint and a curl of her mouth that showed a lack of sympathy for my plight and only contempt for my display of emotion before the king and the crowd. She was obviously embarrassed by the crippled nephew being assisted by the king's charity.

King David then called for Ziba to step forward. The man's goat-face was flushed, his toothless grimace attempting to show deference towards the king, but I saw it for what it was. The man was witnessing his plans falling apart around him, and he was helpless to do anything about it. The king told him, "Since Mephibosheth is Saul's grandson, I'm declaring him Saul's heir. I've given him back everything that belonged to your master Saul and his family. You and your fifteen sons and twenty servants will work for Mephibosheth." Again the loud whispers ran through the crowd. I could tell Ziba was about to become apoplectic. Yet, David was not finished. "You will farm his land and bring in his crops, so that Saul's family and servants will have food. But Mephibosheth," and David looked at me lovingly, patting my knee, "Mephibosheth will always eat with me, at my table." The assembled crowd murmured appreciatively. And then the kind king smiled at me again.

Ziba could do nothing but reply, in a voice empty of emotion and with a face as red as crimson, "Your Majesty, I will do exactly what you tell me to do." From that moment on, Ziba became my sworn enemy because of the hatred in his heart, and he waited for his chance to harm me and take back what he felt was rightfully his, even if it would take him years to do so. "Mephibosheth," I thought, "You have an enemy." In a lifetime filled with potential enemies, this was the first time an actual enemy of mine had a face. However and incredibly, because of the presence and love of King David, I had no fear.

EIGHT

Ariella could hardly believe our great good fortune. She told me that when the wagon arrived from Jerusalem to retrieve her and Michah and our meager goods she had already resigned herself to being a widow for the rest of her life. She and my grandmother and the other women of our family, all of whom had dressed in mourning for what they thought was my impending death, threw off the funereal garb and danced for joy. The news was a great gift from Hashem to them all. Even Machir, who was usually impassive, brought wine out and shared it with all who passed. Perhaps he was glad to be rid of the extra baggage he had carried for so long. Ah, again, I speak ill of him who did me so much good, and I should not.

When the small train of mules and goods was still not quite inside the gates of Jerusalem, Ariella jumped down from the wagon, put our son on the ground, and ran to me at the gate of King David's house. I had asked David to allow me to wait for her there, and he gladly granted my wish. She knelt to hug me as I sat on the chair the King provided for me while I awaited her arrival. We held on to each other for a long time, tears of joy intermingling as the servants began unloading what little we had. Michah, only then walking, tottered and sat on the ground next to us. I'm sure we made for another embarrassing moment for Aunt Michal if she were to see. I did notice that the King saw us from the balcony at his rooms two stories above us, and he turned back from the window after a quick, small wave of his hand and a smile.

After allowing us relative privacy and appropriate time for our tearful reunion, King David came downstairs and stood in the arch behind us where the carts would pass into the inner courtyard of the house. He seemed to be interested in meeting my family for himself, but he did not want to appear to be inappropriate. It was almost as if the King were shy. It was Ariella who noticed him first. Raising her eyebrows, she nodded towards him, and I turned.

"My King," I said, holding my hand out in presentation, "I would like to present my wife Ariella, the daughter of my previous benefactor, Machir, the son of Ammiel."

"I would be honored," David replied, "I know her family well," and he strode across the small courtyard to greet her. She bowed before him in proper fashion, but David asked her to stop.

"You need not do that for me, Ariella," the King said. His forwardness shocked us both. It was not at all the practice then—and still is not in some quarters today—for a man not of our family to directly address a woman, much less another man's wife. David saw our discomfiture and continued.

"My apologies to you and your wife, Mephibosheth. It's only that, well, you are all now of my own…" (The King paused; he had almost said "family") "…household," he said, "and as such, the liberty I am taking is one of a nature I have felt in my heart for you and your…" (He paused again, covering it with a swallow) "…family since before you were born. My intimacy is not from knowledge, admittedly, but rather from a sense of gratitude and remembrance."

He then bent down and scooped up Michah as if he were a puppy and threw him across a shoulder. "Hello, there, my good man!" David said to him as the boy giggled in delight. From the horrified look on her face, I half thought Ariella would reach up and try to snatch her son away from this tall stranger who refused to stand on protocol.

"We are your servants, my Lord" I said in reply, and I meant it.

"No, no!" the King countered, a little sternly but with a smile, as he set Michah back to earth. "For now, let us not worry with formalities. Ask of me what you or your wife needs, and I will see it done. We are not too ceremonial here. If I offend, please know it is not with intent. You and your family are welcome here, always." Finally, he said, "Let us find joy in that and in Hashem." I would come to know that this man pursued Hashem's heart in all things. The King's words, almost poetry to our ears on this and other occasions, brought great smiles to all our faces, and this, in turn, caused the King to reflect that joy.

So, King David made a place in his house for us, giving over three large rooms to our use. Our old house in Lo-Debar could have easily rested in any one of them. Ariella, Hashem bless her, did not know what to do with all that space. In the end, we used only two of the three rooms for ourselves. David also gave Ariella two servant girls of her own; Jordana, the older one, to assist her in the rooms and Sheera, the younger one, to help her with Michah. I was given a manservant, Mordechai, a young man only two years younger than I was. He had fought with King David in the past and had injured his left arm in battle; as a result, he had limited use of that hand. The king, knowing the value of a man is not measured in his body but in his heart, found a place in his household where Mordechai, who still wished to serve both King and God, could still do so. This man not only excelled at knowing court protocol and the position of each person, but he also had training as a doctor and made poultices and potions for my pain. Not having had friends as a child, Mordechai became as close to a friend as I would ever know. We two men, one with bad legs and one with a bad arm, were also united by a love of and for our King.

King David told me to ask if I needed anything and, after speaking to Mordechai, who said it should be no trouble, I did ask for and receive a permanent scribe of my own so I could continue my learning. When he found that I had a great interest in writing and learning, the king ordered Shemaiah, his chief scribe, to give me free roam of his growing archives. Nothing was denied me and, I daresay, short of giving me the crown, which I never desired, King David would have done all he could to meet my every wish. Such was his generosity and such was the joy he derived from giving.

Upon hearing that my grandmother still lived, King David saw to it that she and her two servant girls were given a small but comfortable house on the family's property in Benjamin, not too far away. There she lived until she died, as grateful to Hashem and King David as a daughter of Israel should be, despite the tragedies that haunted her memories and those that still lay ahead for her little family. Ziba did well by her, I must admit, providing her with what she needed, even if he did it with spite in his voice and heart. Perhaps he knew that David watched him closely because of me.

Of Ziba, I saw little—or as little as he needed to be seen. He followed King David's orders and continued to maintain the lands of my grandfather. He dutifully sent shipments of crops and animals to the king's house, inventory that went to the general larder for use by the entire household. He also sent one tenth of all to the Levites as Moses requires. In this, also, I cannot fault him. Every quarter, I received a report from him on the land, the tenants, the taxes, the harvest and the flocks. The first few times, Ziba himself came and reported to me in curt, quick tones, reporting out of obligation's sake rather than information's. We never spoke about any other issues. After a few such meetings, he sent one of his sons to report. I think he wanted to see for himself how I fared in the king's house and, when he saw that I had become a permanent part of the court, he saw no need to speak to someone like myself who was so obviously beneath him.

Soon, we settled into a routine at the King's house—routine at least for us. We still rose early, as was our custom at Lo-Debar, although most of those in the household kept to their rooms until much later in the day. We always found things to do to occupy our time until the rest of the house stirred. The city noises were unsettling to us at first, but we slowly grew accustomed to the flow of life there. Ariella and her servant girls usually went downstairs and brought an early meal to our quarters but, as David had said, every evening meal was eaten in the large dining hall with the king and his men. The men ate at the large table, including the king's sons who were of age and many of his army companions and generals. The women—at times a wife or two of the king—ate at side tables, reclining and overseeing the serving of the men alternately. I can recall only a handful of times that Ariella ate there, outside of the festivals when her absence would have been an affront. The last time she ate in the King's hall, my Aunt Michal made a loud remark that all could hear about crude country women and their lack of fashion—she, Michal, who milked goats before she could walk—all aimed at Ariella. Later that night, in our rooms, my good wife, with tears, swore off ever returning to that table save at the request of the King.

My presence at the king's table was remarkable at first, as is the addition of any newcomer, but soon, as time passed, I was not noticed or seen as being usual. The king always drank at supper, sometimes to the point of shining, but never to the point that he was not himself. His general, Joab, drank as if each meal were his last. Some of the king's sons did as well. Wine never held power over me; I know it, and can drink it, but I have always preferred it well watered. When he shone, the king would tell stories and, without my asking, he would usually tell stories about my father. Oh, how I relished those nights! How I wished them never to end! Some of the tales were of my grandfather, but these were not usual. Some nights, I would look up from my bowl to see the king looking at me with a soft smile. I came to know that he was looking for my father in my face. This became a good and constant reminder that the life I lived before the king and before Hashem was not only my own, but it also reflected on the life of the good father that I never had a chance to know well.

On a rare occasion, an old man joined our meals. He was the prophet Nathan. My children, like many men of Hashem, he wore a full cloak of camel hair, kept his hair long and unclean, his beard streaked and haggard, but his eyes pierced the hearts of all upon whom they fell. Once, a young soldier from King David's tribe sat with us at meal, a young man who should have known better (but what young man knows when to keep his tongue?), and he began to tease the prophet, likening him to a wild beast. The rest of the men at the table immediately fell silent and stopped eating. The king called the young man's name. "Noam! You do not know the nest of hornets you stir!" Noam's head fell to his chest in shame while Nathan's eyes burned at him. According to what we heard later, the next day this young man, Noam, with no warning or reason, simply fell from his mule during an afternoon ride and his head hit a large rock. It crushed his skull and he died instantly. No one wanted to help take the body until the King himself jumped down and put the young man's lifeless form on his own animal. He ordered that the body be sent to Bethlehem, to Noam's father's village, along with money to the family for a proper burial.

The next time the prophet Nathan sat at the king's table, few words were said among the group. No one would look at Nathan and many made a sign of luck when the prophet took his seat. The men on either side of him hardly touched their suppers. For my part, the prophet scared me even more. Ariella always avoided him when she saw him in the house to the point that she would turn on her heels and walk away briskly, also making a sign of luck as she turned. As I made my way more slowly, I could not escape him as easily. One day he spoke to me:

"Son of Jonathan!" he bellowed, appearing beside me suddenly. My crutches slipped in fright as I jumped at the sound of his voice.

"Y-yes?" I managed.

"No pasture! No pasture!" Nathan yelled, his bearded face close to mine, his crooked, yellowed teeth laughing. He walked on past me, still saying, "No pasture!" over and over loudly and to no one. It took me a moment to understand his odd statement. Lo-Debar. The name meant, "No pasture".

We had one other great surprise to happen to us soon after arriving at the King's house. Sitting with Ariella and Michah in our rooms one afternoon, a rasp came on the doorframe outside. The younger servant girl jumped up to see who it was. In walked a beautiful woman with face that looked so familiar, yet not quite placed in my mind.

"Ariella!" the woman said, "My darling niece!" I sat, stunned, as Ariella rose quickly to embrace the younger sister of her father, whom she had not seen for years. This was the laughing girl who had tickled me and made such an impression on me all those years ago.

"Don't you recognize me, Mephibosheth," she teased, smilingly, turning towards me.

"Yes!" I said. "It is good to see you again."

"Uriah told me the King brought you to his house, so I had to come see for myself. I can't believe it! We are neighbors, you know. I live practically next door," she explained. Ariella gave her aunt another sideways hug and beamed,

"I can't believe it either! Isn't it wonderful, Mephibosheth? You know, she is so much closer to my age than to father's. We're practically sisters!"

"Yes," I agreed flatly. "It is wonderful to live so close to you." I was stunned that it was actually Ariella's aunt, here, in Jerusalem with us.

"We have many years to catch up on," Ariella said. "It's been too long, Bathsheba!"

King David was at the peak of his power at that time, my children. His kingdom was at peace. He had found a good hill-city to call his capital. His people loved him. Hashem loved him. He had been born a shepherd in Bethlehem, the youngest son of Jesse, and now ruled a happy, loyal people and controlled a vital trade route between the great land of Egypt to the south and the ancient and powerful Chaldean lands to the King of Kings. Nothing would have pleased King David more than to build a great temple for Hashem—such was David's love for his God. That task would be denied David; it would fall to his son, Solomon, to complete the temple that stands now in the city.

A man who loved and was loved so passionately—such a man as this—had a weakness, as do all men. To be in such complete control over most things in his life, the king still had no control over one rather large and important aspect of it. It was rare for me to see my Aunt Michal at that time. She had been barren ever since she had scolded King David for celebrating before the Ark of Agreement as it was brought into the city. David's wish to have a child that shared his and Jonathan's blood was denied by Hashem. If I encountered Michal with a servant or two in the halls as I slowly made my way to the archives or to or from our rooms, she would quickly speak a greeting and then move on rapidly, pulling her dress out of my way as if my very presence would leave some sort of stain on her finery. I never saw her with the king aside from an occasional religious festival, and then she was only one of several wives present.

One thing King David did well was to keep the disparate parts of his personal life separate, even if his personal life was one of his weaknesses—weaknesses that all men have. Each of his wives had her own small house or rooms within his house; each had a separate set of servants. As I have said, they sometimes came together for meals or celebrations, but this was the exception rather than the rule. As the numbers of his wives grew, so did the numbers of his children. By the time we moved to Jerusalem, the king already had many sons and daughters older than I. Perhaps a man as passionate as King David found that such passion could be found in all parts of his being. Perhaps that is why David married so many women and kept so many concubines. Like it is with wine, I am spared this as well. Ariella's love filled me completely.

No one woman filled King David—until he pursued Bathsheba.

NINE

Ziba, I found out later, was poisoning the well against me with anyone who would listen in the King's household. At that time, if the king heard anything about it, which I'm sure he did, he never betrayed that to me. According to what we heard, Ziba referred to me derisively as, "The Cripple." Being as unfamiliar with life at the King's court as we were, Ariella worried that we could be put out of the King's house at any time for any infraction or none. She often scolded Michah to stay quiet lest we upset the King or one of his court. "What would we do if we were put out? I don't know if father would take us back!" she asked almost tearfully one evening in our rooms. With more fear in my heart then I showed in my voice I reassured her that we would be safe as long as the King did not believe Ziba's falsehoods. I showed her the ring again and recalled David's promises for her. It stilled her soul for that evening. But I could see the worry in her eyes almost constantly. I prayed she never saw it in mine.

The rents from the land and the produce that Hashem gave from it provided us a good living. That money and those goods went over and above the incredible generosity King David showed our family daily. At first, I trusted Ziba's recordkeeping simply because I did not want to cause any disturbance in the household. I certainly did not want to bring any complaint against him before the King. Who was I to question the generosity of both King and Hashem? Yet, as I began looking at the records, and after speaking to Mordechai and one of the King's husbandmen, I began to suspect that Ziba was taking some of the profit for himself. Indeed, he earned a decent living by managing the lands and, besides, he also had his own large landholding that he and his sons oversaw; by itself, his own familial holdings produced a tidy sum for him every year. So, despite my suspicions, I never confided them to anyone save Mordechai. My family and I had grown up being used to living simply. We never quite developed a taste for the finer things in life. Why should we? We had life. We had each other. We had a loving King.

We had Hashem.

Imagine! To go from "no pasture" to living in the King's house in a few months! Surely, Hashem's hand was in it all. And King David reminded me of this in a beautiful and almost miraculous way. In the evenings before we supped, the king enjoyed spending time on the roof of his house, surveying his capital city, seeing the surrounding hills with their olive groves and neatly tended farms. It was here in the gloaming that he often continued to compose his songs for Hashem, a habit that began for him as a shepherd boy, to pass the time while he watched his father's flocks in the hills of Bethlehem. As he reclined on his couches, a plate of figs nearby, he would play the small lyre and sing in what was still a very passable voice for a man his age. Most often, he had a scribe with him who would write what the king played and sang and take it to Heman and Jeduthun, the court musicians, for polishing. The king loved to hear his pieces for large harp and the lyre played in the court and often in the Tabernacle or at festivals.

Who has not heard them? They are played and sung still to this day. King Solomon has collected several of these in the archives, and there they remain fresh for the people of Israel for all time. They are the testimony of a glorious heart that was tuned to the love of Hashem.

It was here on the roof, as the King tuned a string or was thinking of a line, that I began to make my way in the evenings to enjoy the cool of the day and to find the king, unhurried, and engage him in conversation. He liked seeing the smoke from the evening sacrifices from the Tent of Agreement rise slowly to Hashem, and he used his voice to accompany that sacrificial smoke. Much of what we learned from each other—I about my father, and he about my life—found seed in these moments. It was here that I confessed to him of my fears when he first summoned me, and King David expressed surprise at this.

"Ziba did not tell you my purpose for summoning you?" he asked, looking up from his strings. It would still do me no good to speak ill of Ziba; the king might think me little of heart as well as body.

"I am speaking of the first, my King, and before that, when our family only knew of fear." He seemed satisfied with that answer. I quickly continued.

"We felt fear because of the things we had seen and heard since Mt. Gilboa." The King winced slightly at the thought and turned his head sideways as he seemed to examine the strings of the lyre closely. I had heard his wonderfully beautiful song written in my father's honor, "The Bow," in which King David's heart laments the death of his dear companion. It was from this song that I first knew of the depths of the love they shared, the love that would bring me to the King's table and his side. I knew the pain of losing my father hurt him in ways I would never know and hurt him still. David carried the pain of my father's loss until he died.

"I understand," he said finally, seemingly satisfied with the sound of the instrument.

"Besides," I said, "We felt somewhat cursed. We were living in Lo-Debar in poor conditions, relying on the patience and largesse of Machir. Who knew how long that would endure?"

"Lo-Debar," he repeated. "No pasture—is that right?" He looked at me sideways when he said this, a small smile at the corners of his mouth. I returned it. He must have heard about the Prophet Nathan's outburst to me. Of course he had heard; nothing gets by a king in his own house.

"But I have a pasture, now, my King," I said, moving my hand around me. "And, with thanks to you, I have a shepherd." He smiled more broadly now and, instead of answering me, began to sing his song of victory over his enemies:

The Lord is my rock, my fortress and my deliverer; my God is my rock, in whom I take refuge, my shield and the horn of my salvation.

The next evening, by the time I reached the roof, the king sat ready with the lyre. No scribe sat with him; no servant stood. It occurred to me that I had never been the only one in the presence of the king before.

He called, "Mephibosheth! I have been waiting for you. Come, sit over here next to me." I made my way over to the couch next to where he sat and dropped down onto the cushions beside him. Was I being too familiar with such a one? Any questions of impropriety were brushed aside by the king quickly.

"I have a surprise for you," he smiled after I found my seat. "Remember what you said last night?" I did not. He reminded me. "You said you have found a shepherd. I fear you meant me."

"Oh, my king," I said, quickly, "Yes! You have been like a shepherd to me and my family."

He frowned at me. "No, not I, my son. Hashem is your shepherd." And he began to strum the lyre and threw his head back and began to sing this song:

God, you are my shepherd! I will lack for nothing. You have bedded me down in pastures of tender grass.

You find me quiet pools of good water to drink from. You let me catch my breath and send me in the right direction.

Even when life goes through Death's valley I am not afraid because You walk at my side. Your shepherd's crook makes me feel secure.

You serve me a feast-dinner right in front of my enemies. You lift my drooping head, and my cup is filled to the rim with blessing.

Your goodness and love, they chase after me every day of my life. You bring me safely back home to the house of God for the rest of my life.

By the time he had finished, tears washed down my face in great streams. The king touched the top of my head gently, pushing the wet hair back from my eyes. I could see his own eyes glistening with tears as well.

"That song—so beautiful!" I gushed. "Yes! Hashem is truly my Shepherd! There can be no other!"

"Yes," David said. "I'm so glad you liked it, Mephibosheth. I wrote it for you. Never forget," he said, looking out over the rooftops of Jerusalem, "Hashem is your shepherd. I am only a man."

TEN

Bathsheba, the mother of the great King Solomon and aunt of my beloved wife, deserves better than what I am about to write. Yet, I want you, my children, to know the story of how she came to be in the life of King David and how that relationship between them affected us.

As I said, Bathsheba's husband, the Hittite Uriah, was one of David's mighty men. Thus, Bathsheba was someone well known throughout the King's court. She, who would be the mother of one king and the wife of another, was no stranger to the palace or the capital city. Her brother Machir, my father-in-law and former host, had been a mighty man of valor in his day, a man whose reputation still carried some heft. The foreign husband Bathsheba who brought to court had also come to believe Hashem as the great King above all Gods. The King trusted him. So to say that Uriah's wife was an unknown person, as some do today, is simply not true. Perhaps the official record wishes to distance King David from her but, knowing his delight in all things beautiful, he would certainly have known her. Before she became the wife of King David, even I, who usually did not notice such things, saw her beauty for what it was, and had seen it even as a boy. One could not help but notice it. Her beauty wrought envy among women and no little excitement among men. Ariella's beauty was different than that of her aunt; to me, Ariella remains the most beautiful woman Hashem has yet formed from dust. But Bathsheba was beautiful, and to deny it is to lie.

The official records handle the situation with some delicacy. Any other king would never include such intimate details of his personal life in an official document, but not King David. He wished that the story of his poor choices would teach other generations about seeking those things of Hashem above those things of one's own desires. The official story says he saw her from the roof of his house, the same roof where he and I sat that evening when he played the song he wrote for me. Perhaps the idea of looking over his city and seeing her taking a bath is as good a metaphor as any for the way he desired her and brought her to himself.

Most of the rest of the official story is as it happened, since I have heard the story from both sides. It really begins, however, before David brought Bathsheba to his quarters. In the planting season of that year, the king decided not to join his troops in going to war. This caused some concern among the troops and the court. Never before had the king not joined his troops at war; it was he who was always on the front line of any battle. David had never asked his mighty men to do something that he, himself, would be unwilling to do. The resulting rumors in the King's house among the staff said that he was going soft, that he had come to enjoy life and the palace too much. To be fair, that is possibly true. King David was beyond middle-aged at this point. Perhaps he was tired of war. His reasons for not going that year were never told to me. He may not even have known the reasons himself. And, for the purposes of what happened later, the reasons really do not matter. Thus, it was while he was home and his troops were in the field that King David sought to conquer the heart of another man's wife. And, as with most things in his life, he was victorious in this. Who could withstand his charms?

My part in this story is omitted from the official record, and for that I am grateful. Perhaps the King wished to spare me any possible culpability in the matter. My part began with the fact that I felt obligated to the King to do anything for the man who had done so much for me and my family. So, when King David asked me about my wife's aunt, I told him what I knew—which was not much. However, the King then asked me if Bathsheba would take the Passover meal with Ariella and me since her husband, Uriah, was still at war. I had not considered the idea. While he did not directly ask me to invite Bathsheba to dine with us, King David did plant the idea in my head. It was not his nature to ask for a favor but, looking back on it now, it seems that this is what the King asked of me. In any case, he used the invitation to his own ends. I mentioned it to Ariella, and she said the idea was wonderful. She had not celebrated a Passover with Bathsheba in years. She sent the older servant girl to Bathsheba's house with the invitation. Bathsheba sent word back by the girl that she would be honored to celebrate with us. She agreed to come dine on the evening before the holy day sundown.

When the time came, however, Bathsheba never arrived to our rooms. Ariella had asked for a simple but nice Passover meal to be prepared for us in our quarters, and she and the girls had spent the greater part of two days getting the rooms cleaned and readied. They made several trips up and down the stairs to the kitchens, and they brought the food to our rooms and set it all out. I had never hosted a Passover meal before, but I knew the rituals and was ready. So, we five—Ariella, Michah, the two servant girls and I—waited in vain for our guest. As it grew dark, Ariella sent the older girl with a lamp to Bathsheba's house to see if she were sick or if she had any problems that prevented her from joining us.

After the girl returned, she reported to Ariella, "There was no answer at her door, mistress."

This worried Ariella. "Did you knock, loudly?" she asked the girl.

"Yes, mistress. I even called out. Not even a servant answered."

Ariella said to me, "Should we tell someone in the household?"

Before I could answer, the girl spoke up. "Oh, I saw mistress's aunt!"

We exchanged confused looks. "What? I thought you said she wasn't home?" Ariella said.

"No, mistress. I didn't see her at home," the girl said. "I saw her leaving the King's rooms as I was returning."

"Ah," I said, "So, she is not sick. That is good. Shall we begin?" I asked, as Ariella and the girls sank back down in their chairs.

But Ariella was not satisfied. "The King's rooms?" she asked, rhetorically. "Why would she go there?" Her hand moved to her mouth in worry as I saw the first thought come to her. "Oh, no! Maybe her husband, Uriah, has been slain in battle! Perhaps he is injured! The King told her the news himself. She will be in distress. I must go to her!" Ariella exclaimed, standing suddenly.

"Oh, no, mistress!" the girl volunteered, looking up from the table. "My mistress's aunt was not in distress at all when I saw her."

The episode suddenly seemed clear to me. David's interest in Bathsheba was more than our asking her to Passover. I stopped Ariella by touching her hand. "My wife," I said to her, softly, "Please sit down. In the King's house, what happens in the King's rooms is the King's business. We will send to see if your aunt is well after we eat." Ariella slowly sat down as the second thought crossed her mind. She wrinkled her brow as she pondered the situation. We ate that first Passover in Jerusalem in a somber mood.

By early summer, Bathsheba came to be with child by the King. And King David sought to conceal his sin. Her husband, Uriah, this man from another country, came home on leave from the army about that time. Joab, the King's general, often sent officers back with reports for David and, besides, the men needed time away from the fighting. The war had been a particularly difficult one that year. Uriah had injuries, but the injuries would not keep him out of the fighting. Joab wanted Uriah to get rest for the remainder of the campaign that would happen that summer. That night at supper, King David told Uriah that the officer deserved to go home and lie with his wife. David said it to Uriah casually, as if the King were giving his approval to the union and offering a blessing upon it. I know this because I was at table when he said it. However, being the good soldier he was, Uriah, with respect, told the king that he could not in good conscience do so for the army was at war and he wished to save his strength to do battle for Hashem's glory. His pledge before God and King brought shouts of approval and not a few slaps on the back from the others at the long dining table. Even I raised my cup to Uriah's faithfulness. King David looked perplexed. Looking back on it all, and knowing what I know now, it was perhaps the only time I can remember that another man acted better before Hashem than did King David.

Leaving the table that evening, the Prophet Nathan called to me as I made my way down the corridor towards the stairs.

"Son of Jonathan!" he thundered from behind me. I slowly turned on my crutches, but the prophet did not wait for me to face him. "What is your part in this shameful thing?"

"My... my part?" I repeated stupidly.

"Yes!" Nathan said. "You blindly do whatever the King says for you to do. Whom do you serve, son of Jonathan? Hashem or David?"

I was still unclear about what the prophet meant about my part, but I knew what he meant by "shameful thing." "Yes, it is shameful, Prophet," I said to Nathan, in one of the few times my voice found itself in his presence. "But Hashem is merciful."

"Yes," the old man said, softening somewhat as he pondered my response. "Yes. May Hashem have mercy."

He turned and left me alone, and I began the painful climb up the stairs to our rooms. Ariella and I suspected what had happened that Passover eve, but we never referred to it directly. Such things might be talked about today, but in our day it was not so. Ariella had asked her aunt about it some weeks later, apparently, but all Bathsheba would confirm to Ariella was that she was indeed with child.

Shameful. That was the word Nathan used. My confusion was that what King David did all throughout the situation was uncharacteristically selfish—the lust, the adultery, the murder, all of it. He who was one of the most unselfish men I ever met had acted in one of the most selfish ways I have ever known. When Uriah finally returned to his unit on the front lines of the war, King David gave him a pouch with sealed messages for his army leaders. Poor Uriah! For he did not realize that he carried with him a message to the army commander, the great general Joab—his own death warrant. A copy of that message rests in the royal archives even today; if you wish to know what that message said, children, read it for yourselves.

My children, even though these events took place so many years ago, my heart is still heavy with the sadness that these poor choices brought on many families, many lives, the king himself, the people of Israel, and our own poor selves! For you know the rest of this sordid tale. Uriah was truly murdered by his own king. Even the lives of other soldiers were lost in this "shameful thing" as part of the King's effort to cover up his crime. Much of Israel lost respect for David when all was revealed. Certainly the wives and the children and the families of the men who died on account of David's lust lost respect for him.

So, the news finally did come that Uriah, my uncle-in-law, was dead in battle. His wife, Bathsheba, observed mourning dress and demeanor for the proper time and in the proper way. When the traditional mourning period ended, Bathsheba promptly closed her house and moved into the King's house. David took her as his wife. She rarely left his side for the rest of his life. If he regretted his choice of Bathsheba, King David never said so to me. Yet, the harshest result of all these poor choices, at least in the King's eyes, was how they damaged his relationship with Hashem.

My own sins should give me pause, as well. A man knows, my sons, when he sins before the Lord—especially the man whose relationship with his God is as David's relationship was. Such a man does not always need a prophet to tell him Hashem is saddened by his sin. However, a lesser man than David would never have admitted his wrong. May Hashem continue to give us rulers who acknowledge their sins before Him! May we always seek Hashem's mercy and forgiveness! I will say this, and it comes from the mouth of King David himself. He sinned against and before Hashem. Hashem does not want our sacrifices. He does not need our tithes. Anyone can make those and not have the smallest bit of shame or sadness over his sin. What Hashem wants is a heart that is broken before Him. That is true for all of us and for all of our sins—David's and mine, and your sins, too, my children. Remember that when you go to the temple and make your prayers.

It was the prophet Nathan who first confronted the King about his sin. And, as a man of God, King David repented. A lesser man would have taken the head of the one who caught him in a wrong. Not so King David. He went into mourning for his crime against Hashem, going as far as putting on sackcloth and ashes to show his repentance. The child Bathsheba birthed died shortly after coming into the world; it was a child of sin, if there ever was one. Afterward, David threw off the mourning clothes and became somewhat more like himself again. Bathsheba never wore the label of "shameful" long.

Those who talked about it overlong among themselves found they were in the small minority. She soon became as much a part of life in the King's house as the kitchen, the throne room, or the stable, and more involved in the day-to-day life of the King than any wife he ever had.

All of this I viewed from afar as the King had other, much more important issues on his mind than me. But one heard the stories in such a relatively small house. Some of this I even heard from Nathan in later years. Some of it I heard from Bathsheba herself. After the loss of that first child, it was soon announced that Bathsheba was once again with child. This time, there was great rejoicing at the announcement. And I was honored to be among the group who stood outside the queen's bedrooms when it was announced that she gave birth to the son who would become King Solomon. The prophet Nathan, upon hearing the news of the birth of a son, came behind me as I stood balanced on my crutches; he almost knocked me over with a hearty slap on my back. "A son! What do you think of that, No Pasture?" Recovering from my shock, I stuttered, "Hash—Hashem be praised, Prophet! May he be beloved of God." Nathan's eyes drew together in a squint as he looked at me and turned the phrase over in his head. "Indeed! Beloved of God he shall be!"

At that moment, King David came out of the room where his wife lay. In his arms was a tiny, red, shriveled and wrinkled baby boy. The child had a slender frame and his hair was dark like his mother's. The small gathering cooed and sighed appreciatively.

The prophet Nathan approached the King. "Have you chosen a name?" he demanded.

"I was thinking Solomon," King David said, smiling at the child.

"Yes, yes," the Prophet replied, turning the name over on his tongue. "Solomon. Solomon. That will do," he said, turning to leave us. From over his shoulder he added, as he strode away, "For now."

ELEVEN

King David's life was never the same after that. True, the child Solomon became a great comfort to him, a source and sign of peace between him and Hashem, but David's run of good fortune ended with that conquest of Bathsheba. What had been a long series of great successes turned into disaster upon disaster for the King's family and for his people. It is as if the King were driving a great wagon at high speed, only to have all the wheels come off it at the same time. Yes, the more superstitious among you would say that Hashem punished the king for his great sin. Both David and Nathan, however, saw it differently. Nathan told the king that God had forgiven him for the sin because of David's contrition. The King never doubted that. No, what happened for the rest of the King's life was not punishment. But the Lord has a way of reminding us of who we are and Whose we are, dear children. And I believe firmly that the difficulties the King faced for the rest of his life acted as God's reminders on David's heart. I can, these many years later, still vividly remember my dear grandmother tugging my ear when I chose poorly as a child. David's difficulties in his later life were Hashem's way of tugging on David's ear.

Of all of the King's wives, Bathsheba now replaced all of them at his side, as I have said. His love for her was great. Perhaps he knew how much she had cost him, and one keeps someone so dear close to one. Also, as I have said, this is the single part of his life which I never understood about King David. He had proved himself correct; he was but a man. Yet, having Bathsheba close to him meant that my interactions with her became more and more frequent. Over the years, she became, in many ways, like an older sister to me as well as my wife's aunt and King David's wife. Perhaps it was because, as a relative by marriage, I was seen as no threat to David, and therefore I was allowed to speak freely to Bathsheba and she allowed to speak freely to me. While Bathsheba grew to be the sister in my life that I never had, King David never seemed to me to be my brother; he always seemed so much more like a father. Perhaps that was because Bathsheba was much nearer in age to me than I was to the King.

She would often join him on the rooftop in the evenings from that point on, something the other wives would never dream of doing. Soon, she came to be expected; where the King went, so went his Queen. The rooftop evenings were where she and I first began our tentative conversations with each other. She always seemed bird-happy, while I tend to be more taciturn and shy. Despite this difference, we realized early on that we shared many things in common besides being members of the same extended family. In many ways we were both outsiders. She was the object of much scorn among many in the household, especially the other wives. And I was an outcast because of who I was and the fact that I was a cripple, thus most of the other men in the court had little use for me. Yes, that drew us to each other as friends—that and our devotion to David. After some months we began speaking more freely, as the king seem to play and sing less and less and Bathsheba and I talked more and more to fill the silence. As I said, he was changed. For a man who was so robust for so long, he began in less than a year to show his age. Gone was any trace of the rust-colored hair he had worn long for so many years. Now a gray-headed man, the King asked his servants to keep his hair shorter.

Ah, my beloved Ariella, my dear one! For if she harbored any jealousy over the amount of time my friendship with Bathsheba took away from my time with her and my son, to her credit she never revealed it. Perhaps she knew that having such a friend and sister who was as close to the king as Bathsheba was could prove to be to our benefit. She was, as always, worried about our situation. Such was her nature. For my part, I had found a friend who had a curious and sharp mind. Bathsheba, I soon learned, was a keen judge of character. Her instinct as given to her by Hashem proved invaluable in helping me navigate the intricacies of court life. While most of the other wives of David, including my Aunt Michal, were intriguing against her or worried about their fading looks or how to gain David's attention, Bathsheba, whose beauty never faded, even in old age, grew secure in her relationship with the king. She knew how much the King loved her. She understood his obligation to the other wives, and it never seemed to bother her when he would pay his visits to their bedrooms. She knew he would always come back to hers as his home. She also came, over time, to reinforce in my heart how much the King loved me and my family. Of course, I had proofs of that love every day. Never a meal passed that the King did not look down the table at me and smile. I noticed that he would stare at me often, continually seeking my father in my features in a smaller, weaker version. I smiled weakly when I saw that he did so, knowing that I was but a pale imitation of my beloved father in the King's eyes. Still, it gladdened my heart that my presence made the King even a little happy.

After we had established our friendship as well as our kinship, Bathsheba would often make her way to the archives, usually trailing an attendant or two but sometimes by herself. There we would look at tablets or scrolls together. Somewhere along the way, she had learned to read a bit, and this surprised me. When I told her so, she laughed. "Do you think women have no brains, Mephibosheth?" she asked. I could see how David found a challenge and also a true companion in her. Next to his God, his people, and my father, Bathsheba was loved by David more than anything else.

Bathsheba convinced David that Nathan should have a great role in the raising of Solomon. The prophet never referred to the child as Solomon. Instead, he insisted upon calling the young man Jedidiah, the name I had inadvertently put in his head at the boy's birth. Soon after the boy's weaning celebration, Nathan's role in the household changed greatly. He was given two rooms at the back of the house, near the stables, where he would tutor the young prince, and he was given two servants to help in the care of the child during the day. The only stipulation Bathsheba put on him—and this must have rankled the old prophet—was that he keep better care of his body. I heard about this later from her, and she laughed when she told me, that Nathan protested strongly to the King, but David agreed with his wife. "It is unseemly for your wife to concern herself over my person!" Nathan had thundered at the King. But Bathsheba would not be moved in this. We were all careful not to comment or stare too closely when Nathan appeared at supper one evening with a neat but obviously self-trimmed beard and a fresh set of ill-fitting clothes. His demeanor changed as well with time. He insisted upon calling Solomon the name I had inadvertently put in his head at the birthing—Jedidiah. Soon, the dread I felt at his presence came to be replaced with a loving respect and awe. We even managed a smile or two between us that I recall.

As you know, children, Nathan wrote two great histories of the reigns of King David and of King Solomon (as much as Hashem allowed him to live to see of Solomon's reign, that is). At the time

I met him, he must have been about the same age as King David, although he seemed infinitely older and yet ageless at the same time. When the mood suited him, Nathan allowed me to sit with him and Solomon as the young man took his lessons. I soon found myself also referring to Solomon as Jedidiah, but I would never think of doing so now. It was obvious from an early age that the lad had a quick mind like his mother and great wisdom like his father. However— and the King agrees with me, by the way—the Great Wise King that Solomon has become happened largely because of the great care with which Nathan taught him the ways of Hashem. Praise be to God!

In the town, when he and Nathan would take walks through the markets and around the walls, the young man usually asked traders and soldiers who had come from far away if they had tablets or scrolls with them they would be willing to trade or sell. He later commissioned traders to seek out books from both the Tigris and Euphrates area and from the valley of the Nile. He became a collector of wisdom sayings of the lands around Israel; the seeds of this collection became the great archives and library of King Solomon in which I now sit.

For a short few years—and things change quickly in life, my children—events at court settled back into a routine. Even my Aunt Michal managed to be less dour in public on those rare occasions she would be seen out of her house. My time was spent in the archives or with Nathan and Solomon by day and, usually, on the rooftops in the evening before the meal. At table, as usual, I would catch the King staring at me, and would still occasionally wonder if I had breached some kind of etiquette that he was too kind to state publicly. When our eyes would meet in those moments, he would brighten and smile, his eyes moist with tears. Yes, for a time things returned to normal.

Then Absalom happened.

TWELVE

Michah, my son, and my beloved four grandsons, you have all been a source of great joy and pride to me. I see in you the tallness of our father's family and the handsomeness of your mother's. Have you been perfect children? No. No such thing exists. Nor do perfect parents exist (unless one counts the love of Hashem!). David was not a perfect parent, either. Some of his children received many of the negative qualities of their mothers and some from their father. We, our little, helpless family, sometimes lay at the mercy of these weak-willed (and, sadly, at times strong-willed) children of King David. The next part of our family's story will tell you of one of those times.

Of all the sons and daughters of King David—and still today they are numerous—none was as headstrong as his son Absalom. While his father may have been "peace," Absalom had no peace in him. From the first time I saw him when he was only a young man, he carried himself as a superior, one above those he considered to be his lessers about him. For example, I was so far beneath him that he gave me no notice; perhaps he saw me as another in a long line of his father's freeloaders, a trait in David that Absalom no doubt saw as a weakness. None of David's kindness lived in him. This arrogance he bore delighted many who met him; people mistook the arrogance in Absalom for David's confidence in Hashem. They could not have been more wrong, for Absalom's confidence sprang not from Hashem but rather it came from himself.

It is true that his mother was a princess—Maacah, the daughter of King Talmai of Geshur. David married Maacah in order to forge a peace (thereby also garnering Absalom his name when he was born). And she had a type of angular beauty that she passed on to her son. She gave her beauty in greater quantities to her daughter Tamar, Absalom's full sister. Absalom, David loved. Ammon, the oldest of the princes, David accepted. Having only one son as I do, my love for you, Michah, is absolute. You, my son, have four boys, and I know you love them all, but they are, after all, different men with different desires and needs. Ammon, the King's first heir, came from a different mother. He grew to be a weak, petty man, easily swayed by his passions. His name meant "faithful," a name he never lived up to. Ammon's faults made him ill-suited to claim the throne that David held. The brothers, both sons of David, separated by only a few years, grew up as rivals in most things, including games, women, and even for the attention of the father they shared. Now, children, I believe that if Ammon's weakness had not spurred Absalom's arrogance and anger, something else would have done so. Thus, I blame Ammon for being a weak man, but the full brunt of the blame for the ultimate result of what happened later must rest with Absalom's pride and hatred and jealousy.

I must speak of Tamar, and I have spoken to hardly anyone else of what I am about to say to you save your beloved mother and grandmother, Ariella. The girl Tamar (She was not a girl, but since she was younger than I was at the time, even today I still think of her as a girl) had received a gift from Hashem of dreams. She could portend events, and I have witnessed such on several occasions, as have many still alive today. Like the rest of the court, I knew her, and knew of her beauty but, for some reason that only Hashem knows, I also provoked strong feelings in her. You may think me forward or inappropriate in the way in which I spoke to Bathsheba, but I never touched her person, even though she was one of our family. The same, I confess, cannot be said of Tamar; or rather, the truth is that she touched me. She remains to this day the only woman or girl outside of our family who, to my knowledge, has done so.

When we celebrated the Festival of First Fruits during our fifth year in Jerusalem, I found my path on the way to the feast table blocked by this young woman, Tamar. Her lovely, dark eyes stared intensely down at me (as you know, children, everyone towers above me, as did even Ariella, as short as she was). Tamar bent slightly and grabbed me by the shoulders, unbalancing me on my crutches. Ariella, walking beside me, reached out to steady me, but Tamar stopped her from doing so with a strong forearm. As I have told you, no woman outside our family ever touched me, and the shock of her firm grasp became magnified when she bent to look in my eyes as she said:

"Son of Jonathan! Do you love the King?" Taken aback by her touch more than her question, I could only stare at her, wide-eyed, and nod meekly. She did not let go. "Do you?" she persisted.

"Yes!" I managed to say, but she did not release her grasp.

"I dreamed of you," she said in a low but firm voice. "I saw you with a long beard, haggard clothing, and unclean feet. You were in mourning."

She looked up then, over my head, to some seemingly distant point. She released me and continued on past us, walking against the flow of the group moving towards the feast. I turned to follow her with my eyes, but by the time I moved around she had vanished in the crowd. Ariella's hand on my elbow brought me back to the moment. We were both stunned into silence by the interaction and looked at each other with wide eyes. I did not know what Tamar meant by what she said until much later. After that, Tamar and I never spoke again until after Ammon took her. I tell you, children, I regret nothing that I did because I said or did nothing improper with her. My regret lies with the ammunition my actions gave Ziba and others in tales they would later take to King David, tales that would wound the King who had been so good to me.

You and all of Israel know the story. Ammon became lost in his passions for Tamar, his half-sister. Knowing what I know now, she must have begged him repeatedly to stop his advances and to listen to reason. Why did she not approach the King with the situation? Ammon, he who could have had any wife in Israel and beyond, became consumed by Tamar and inconsolable when she denied him. I daresay that the King might even have given consent to a marriage if Ammon had approached him in the right manner; such a thing was done more at that time than it is now. However, reason and modesty had no place in his heart. Ammon's passion finally overwhelmed him and, with help from his uncle's son, he first deceived, then took her. His passion slaked, and knowing that his actions violated both his sister and Hashem, he threw her out once he had her, so her great shame doubled.

While some questioned the manner of Ammon's death—the fact that Absalom waited two years for vengeance, using the King's permission to have the princes to his feast for the shearing of the sheep (all the princes went save Solomon, a much younger son and over whom Nathan kept constant vigil), and then sending men to do the murderous work for him so that his own hands, literally, spilled no royal blood—no one blamed Absalom at the time for taking his brother Ammon's life. After all, Tamar shared a mother with Absalom, people reasoned, and he acted as he did to defend not only the honor of his sister but also that of his mother's royal family. No, the act never aroused suspicion among the people. No one, it seems, except his father, liked or even tolerated Ammon at any rate; to a man they preferred the beauty and leadership of Absalom. Such was Absalom's charm over Israel. In this, he mirrored his father.

Absalom's actions convinced me that he saw David's inaction in the matter—the King's reluctance to punish his oldest son and heir—as yet in another long list of signs that David needed to be replaced as king of Israel. His father was too old to rule, he must have thought. Killing Ammon was only the first step that would lead to the throne for Absalom. He personally brought Tamar into his own house after Ammon threw her out. From there, I received word through Mordechai, my servant and friend, that Tamar refused to see anyone. She never left the house. She rarely ate and barely spoke. One servant girl lived with her; other than that interaction, she had no contact with anyone else. After Absalom sought refuge in his grandfather's land and court to escape the wrath of the King, she lived there for some time with the girl who could be seen going to the market on rare days or running a quick, small errand here or there. Tamar became forgotten by almost everyone.

Meanwhile, King David bore double grief: He lost Ammon, the son he had chosen as heir, and he lost Absalom, the son he loved most. The official record says he grieved over Absalom every day—so few words to describe such great sorrow. We saw little of King David for a long while; we still took our meals in the large dining hall, but the King ate in his chambers or in Bathsheba's rooms. When we did see him, he acted as if in a dream or far away. The shock of the death—two deaths, actually, since Absalom left so suddenly after the murder and without any word to the King—dealt a heavy blow to the aging David.

One day, a scrape at the door of the archives where I sat reading revealed the young girl in Tamar's service. Her young eyes filled with wonder at the sight of all the rolls of books on the shelves while my own eyes questioned why she sought me. When asked, she said she brought a message from her mistress for me. The girl said, "My mistress, Tamar, asks that you come to her house tonight, alone, to see her." As she turned to leave, I thanked her without accepting or declining the invitation, and she did not ask for either. When I told Ariella of the summons after supper, she shrank in fear. "Do not go, my husband!" she begged. "Who knows what she wants? What will the King think of you?" Ariella, like many in the court, felt that Tamar's gift of dreams bordered on witchcraft. And my wife knew that appealing to what the King might think of me would pull at my heart strings. Disguising my own trepidation, I assured Ariella that going to Tamar could do us no possible harm; besides, I reasoned, who was I to not do a kindness to someone who asked me when so much kindness had been done to us?

In a rare event, David had been at supper that night, and the sadness in his eyes as he barely touched his food also made me want to see what his daughter needed of me. So, out of a desire to possibly help my King who had been so kind and to help a woman to whom so much wrong and hurt had been done, I had Mordecai fix a small lamp and lead me as quietly as we could go down back streets and alleys to Absalom's house north of the Gihon Spring. When we arrived, I told Mordecai to return home, and I scraped at the door. The servant girl opened it as if she knew all along I would come. She patiently held the door open as I came in the house sideways on my crutches, and then she led me into a small room where I saw Tamar sitting on a couch. The room smelled of stale air, as if no sun had been allowed in for some time. It was as if the house itself suffered from a deep pain.

Oh, children! Tamar was a shell of her former beauty. She wore old, torn, ragged clothing, and kept her hair short like a man. I had never seen a woman with hair like that. Her cheekbones pointed out at me like arrows, and her hands seemed to have no skin on them; they were only flesh-colored bones. On her forehead, she had spread ashes with her grimy hands to symbolize her grief. Who could blame her? She lost her pride and dignity to a brother, and then lost the brother who loved and avenged her by his having to flee the wrath of their father. She had lost the father, too, in a way. She had become sadness. With shrunken eyes, Tamar watched me enter.

In a flat, emotionless voice, she said, "Son of Jonathan. Thank you for coming." She made no mention of whether or not I was to sit, so I shifted on my crutches to take pressure off my legs. She seemed not to notice. "Hashem has left me," she added, looking away from me and down at her dirty hands in her lap.

"Left...you?" I asked. I was not sure what she meant.

"Yes," she answered. "I can no longer dream; I can barely sleep. Hashem is gone from me. How does one answer this? I could not and did not. She continued. "There is one thing in the world I wish."

She let that statement hang in the air, and in the silence I shifted my weight on the crutches and asked her, "What is that wish, Tamar, daughter of David?"

At the sound of her name, she pulled her head up again and looked at me with her dull, gray eyes. "I want my brother, Absalom, back home with me."

At this, it was my turn to look away from her, but I found this difficult. Her eyes, shrunken and dimmed as they were, still held me powerfully, as powerfully as her hands had done on my shoulders at the festival. "That is not something I can do for you, Tamar," I said finally.

"Oh, but you can help me, son of Jonathan," she countered, speaking with more energy now. My eyes came back to her.

"How?" I asked.

"You can talk to the King for me," she offered. "You can tell him that I'm lost without my brother, that I need him here with me. He will listen to you, I know it."

"You overestimate my worth to the King," I protested.

"I think not," she said, looking at me in earnest. "You see, I know about you. I know about the love my father had for yours, and your father for mine. Yes, the King will listen to you."

"Why me?" I asked, still trying to remove myself from her mind. What she was asking is not something one in my position asks of a king.

"Because," she began, her eyes filling with tears, "I have no one else."

Her words struck something in me, children. Perhaps it was knowing what it was like to live in a place both in body and in mind, a place that held no pasture. Having now had such wonderful green pastures given to me by Hashem through King David, perhaps I wished to give some of that pasture to this pitiful creature who had been so wronged. "I'll see what can be done," I said, "but I make to you no oath other than that I will speak to the King for you. I don't know that King David will hear anyone, now."

"That is all I ask," she said, her voice dropping again and her eyes returning to her hands in her lap. "Thank you," she called, somewhat louder, as I turned to leave.

I nodded to her as the servant girl opened the door, and I made my way out. Mordecai had waited for me at the corner of the house. "I asked you to go home," I scolded him gently, him having become more of a friend to me than a servant.

"Yes, I know," he answered, "but we were followed here. I could not see who it was, but as I left you, he ran away. I wanted to stay here and tell you and then help you home with the lamp. The streets are treacherous. By the way, what did Absalom's sister want?" I told him her request, and in the lamplight I saw that he winced slightly.

"The King will be reluctant to hear that request," he said.

"That is what I think as well," I assured him, "but I promised her I would say something. I can do that, at least."

"At most," Mordecai said in a somewhat scolding tone. With that, he turned the lamp towards the next alleyway, and we made our way home.

THIRTEEN

Whoever the person was following us to Tamar's house did not concern me at first. I thought Mordecai might have been mistaken. No, my immediate concentration centered on what and how I would say to King David the thing that Tamar wanted me to ask. One in any position, much less someone like me, could not be so forward with the King as to simply march to his room and make such a request. One does not say such to a grief-stricken man, bringing a message from his disgraced, grieving daughter. No, this would take tact and the right timing, and maybe the help of someone closer to the King than I.

About a week after my meeting with Tamar, I almost tripped over Bathsheba who was entering the archive room as I was leaving it.

"Mephibosheth!" she cried, greeting me as a long-lost relative.

"My Queen!" I responded, nodding my head at her in respect.

"Where are you headed?" she asked, "to your rooms? How is my niece?"

"Ah, she is well, and yes, I'm going to our rooms for a bit. I'm tired today." The truth was that sleep had been eluding me in the past week as I sought for words to say to the King on Tamar's behalf.

"Can you spare me a moment?" she asked, motioning for the girl with her to move away from us down the corridor.

"For you, yes, as much time as you need," I replied. We sat on a bench that lined the wall outside the archives.

"I fear for the King," she began in hushed tones. "He is dying inside over all that has transpired with his sons. It's been three years, Mephibosheth! Three years! And still he grieves."

My words came to my mouth as if they were there all the time. "A King who loves so deeply must grieve deeply as well, my Queen."

She considered my statement. "Yes, you are right," she nodded. "That's why I have a plan." She explained an idea where she would, through a round-about means, show the King that he could ease his pain somewhat by forgiving and bringing back Absalom from his grandfather's court in Geshur.

"I know the king will kick against this," she said, sadly, "but not having it resolved is killing him. You see it, don't you, Mephibosheth?" I agreed.

The official records report that it was General Joab who hatched the plan in King David's mind to bring Prince Absalom back from his grandfather's lands, but the egg of the idea was laid by Bathsheba. After speaking to me about the idea, Bathsheba convinced Joab that having Absalom home would soothe the hurt of losing Ammon. Reluctantly, Joab agreed, even though the general never liked Absalom and saw the young man as a threat to both king and people. So, through the machinations of Bathsheba and Joab, King David allowed the young man to come home, as you know, children. Prince Absalom returned to Jerusalem, and having him closer indeed gave the King some modicum of happiness. Yet, it would be an additional three years before Absalom would be allowed back in the direct presence of King David. The poets say extreme happiness and extreme sadness are brothers of the same mother; apathy is the opposite of both. While the King did not allow his son to see him out of his sadness, I know he did not feel apathetic towards Absalom. I feel he was waiting for the right time, and only Hashem would put that moment on the King's heart.

When they finally met, their joyful crying and kisses were a sight to behold. From beside the throne, Bathsheba's face glowed with happiness and tears for her husband. I know this to be true, for I saw it all. Absalom had returned. His father forgave him. All seemed well. I never had to speak to the King on Tamar's behalf and, in this, Hashem provided for me. The result suited Ariella as well. And Tamar must have been pleased.

The years of exile seemed at first to have matured Absalom somewhat. He settled down a bit; he had sons. Finally, he had a daughter. He named her Tamar. She grew to be a beauty, the favorite of her reclusive aunt who ended up raising her, and she was rumored to have been born with special gifts from Hashem.

FOURTEEN

The seeming maturity that Absalom exhibited upon return from exile served only as a mask for his true intentions. At the end, all he learned during his time away was how to get what he wanted—the throne of Israel—in a more devious manner. This became evident soon after he came back. One of his first acts after he and his father reconciled was to make a daily public display in the marketplace of being one of the common people. He could be seen laughing with the vendors or making free with wine for any and every person who passed by. He encouraged those with grievances against another to come to him—he would see that justice would be done for his friends. And everyone was his friend.

Remember, children, this man stepped into the place that the aging King David had abandoned. No one at that time in Israel held the people's hearts as David had done as a much younger man. Absalom became a younger, if more selfish and devious, version of what his father used to be. Remember, my children, that in the absence of leadership, people will follow anyone who points in a direction. And Absalom pointed at himself. Caught up as we were with our own lives and issues (Ariella first developed the cough that she would eventually carry to her grave during this time, an issue of no small concern to me), I cannot say with certainty when Absalom truly and actively began his attempt to wrest the throne from his father.

Only two generations away from the traditional judges of Israel (the prophet Samuel, as you know, being the last of those great leaders, both men and women), those who knew said Absalom indeed tried to first set himself up as one of their cloth, a person to whom grievances could be legitimately brought and fairly decided. I know for a fact that he also hired men as a sort of bodyguard for his person, men who had the reputation of having a thirst for blood and were quick to anger. That is always a dangerous mixture—ambition and violence.

When I next took notice of him, Absalom had removed himself to Hebron, where the former capital of King David was, and he moved into David's empty house there. Also, Hebron was where a small coterie of Absalom's supporters waited for him, and several more of his supporters in Jerusalem joined him there. I remember it was a time when the days were warming and getting long, so it was early summer. Without warning and, as it later came to light, with much secret agreement among Absalom's confederates in the various tribes of Israel, he struck.

Mordecai had asked my leave to go with Absalom to Hebron simply because many of Absalom's friends had also been his friends when he was a soldier; they were of the same generation and had fought wars with many of them when he had use of both of his arms. It was one of these men who asked Mordecai to go with them. In Mordecai's mind, at least, the group went there to offer sacrifices and to hold a feast. I knew Mordecai well, and to this day I know he bore no sympathy with Absalom; I am certain that he loved the King as I did, so I am convinced of his innocence in this matter.

To prove that to you, my children, it was he who hastened to Jerusalem to warn King David when he saw the way the wind blew in Hebron as Absalom prepared to usurp the throne of Israel. As a former military man himself, Mordecai knew the signs and understood the talk. He managed to slip away in darkness and rode throughout the night to warn the King. He came to me in the early morning and woke me and helped me into the King's rooms, so I was there when he told David what Absalom planned. "The people, my King, they are with Absalom in Hebron," he reported, "and he encourages them to follow him." The look of shock on the King's face, the sheer sadness his visage displayed, will stay with me until Hashem takes my life. The look of betrayal and pain that ran across David's face was worse than the sadness over the Ammon situation. David, old and tired as he was, still listened to the warnings of Mordecai and ordered the household to prepare to flee the city. The house flew into an organized panic as clothing and goods were rolled into carpets and blankets and thrown on wagons and mules. Ariella and I had never accumulated much by way of personal items other than what we needed. With the help of her girls, we were able to be ready quickly, including Michah, who was plenty old enough to put together his own bundle of clothes and belongings. For the second time in my life, my family prepared to flee as a new king sought to take advantage of a situation.

King David left hurriedly, choosing to wear old clothing and to walk barefooted out of the city as a sign of his sadness. I was told that tears streamed from his face over leaving Jerusalem. Or was it over the realization that his beloved son had betrayed him? Or could it be that the old man felt the sting that his own people, the flock he dearly loved, actually loved someone else? Or did he remember what Nathan had prophesied after Bathsheba, that one of his own household would betray him, and that prophecy being fulfilled brought up the remembrance of his poor choices during that period?

Or it could be all of those things. I know it was a sadness that took years of life from my beloved King.

Seeing the state in which David so hurriedly left the city, I made a fateful choice. I sent Mordecai on an errand to fetch Ziba's oldest son who lived near the city with the message that I had an errand for him to do for the King. Ariella, having seen what happens to refugees left behind after a great defeat, and having a clear memory of another time and place and evacuation, tearfully pleaded with me to not wait on Ziba's son but to leave with the King and the train. She invoked Michah and even Hashem, plucking at my own heart with what she knew I loved in an effort to get me to leave. Rest her soul! She feared for me so, always, even until she died. But I determined to stay and help my King in the best way I could. King David had enough to worry over without having to see to my care. How could I do otherwise after what he had done for me? In the end, Ariella and Michah stayed behind with me to wait, as did her two girls. I insisted that Mordecai leave as soon as the message was delivered, and he did so. I convinced him that to be in Jerusalem when Absalom entered the city would be a death sentence, especially if Absalom found out that it was Mordecai who had alerted David to the impending attack. Besides, Mordecai had his own little family, a wife and child, to which he had to see. So he agreed, and left after he informed the son of Ziba that I needed him.

In the stillness of the hall of the King's emptied and abandoned house, Michah sat on his own small parcel, bored after all that flurry of activity while Ariella and her girls stood next to the household bags, the three of them weeping quietly. As for me, I waited for Ziba's son to arrive.

FIFTEEN

At Ziba's son's house, Mordecai found not only the son and his family but also Ziba himself. The man might have been duplicitous but was never stupid. He knew what Absalom was about, possibly long before any of us did. Deceitful people seem to discern each other's motives earlier than others do. When Mordecai gave them the message, Ziba assured him that he, personally, would come to see about me.

That he did. Seeing Ziba after so many months—years, even— would have been shocking in other circumstances. The man had grayed considerably. He had done well by my ancestors' lands as well as his own, and it showed in his clothing as well as his belly. Ziba entered the King's house and called for us. We answered in unison, and he found us easily. He approached us with a smile. My suspicion, which normally would have been aroused, should have noticed that he was charming and eager to assist me in anything—or so he said. He even patted Michah on the head as one would a pet as we spoke.

That accommodating manner should have told me he meant evil. Never had I so much as asked anything of him, so for me to instruct him as to my wishes should have been jolting to Ziba, but he betrayed no emotion through the smile he gave me.

"Take some mules from the property," I began, "and fill their packs with the summer produce. Take the wine and oil also. Meet the King's train with the goods. King David left in such a hurry and has no provision on which to live. He also has no mule for himself. Take a good one, one that is calm, and put the King on it. Offer him money from the treasury of the land, Ziba, hold nothing back, and do not let him refuse. Make sure, also, that Queen Bathsheba has an animal for herself. Do you understand?"

Ziba did not hesitate. He smiled. "Yes, my young lord. It shall be done as you wish." Never had he addressed me as such, but I had no time to notice it then.

"When you have done that, send one of your sons back here for me and my family. We will be waiting. Do not send for us until you have refreshed the King. Agreed?"

"Yes; it shall be as you wish." He bowed slightly, rose with a smile, and hurried out.

Ariella, her tears dried, noticed it first. "He was a bit happy about that, Mephibosheth."

I agreed. "Soon, he will send for us with some mules so we can join the train."

Ariella told the girls they and Michah should go back upstairs and try to rest until Ziba's son returned for us. I agreed, and decided to wait in the hall for him. I sat down on one of the long benches that lined the walls where petitioners to the King used to wait. I stretched out to rest and wait then nodded off, and the next thing I remember, Jordana, the older of Ariella's girls, was standing over me and holding a lamp.

"Sir?" she asked loudly, "my lady wants to know what we should do."

I struggled up into a sitting position. "What?" I asked, still half asleep.

"What should we do? It's night, sir. Michah is...we are all... hungry. What should we do?"

I realized then that Ziba had had plenty of time to do what I asked and still send for us. I then began to realize that perhaps the old fox had tricked me. That is why he smiled. He had no intention of returning.

"What should we do?" the girl repeated.

Getting up and onto my crutches, I told her to go ahead upstairs, that I would be following her. She obeyed, carrying the lamp so I could see. By the time we got up to our rooms I was exhausted. I could see on Ariella's face that she, too, knew that we had been betrayed by Ziba. Michah, much like his mother, could always sense that something was wrong. Perhaps that is the nature of all children. For some reason, I was not panicked, but I could see that Ariella was very nearly so. What I wanted to do was try to keep her calm and also see about the three young ones with us. I told Jordana to go down to the kitchen house and see if there were anything left in the larder for us to eat. She came back in a few minutes with some bread and a little honey that she said had been left out on the table. She had heard noises in other parts of the house, and it frightened her, so she returned to us with all she could grab quickly. We were grateful to Hashem for the food, and we drank some of the water that we had by our beds. With that, I told Ariella and the younger ones to try to sleep. Things could be better assessed in the morning, I told her.

For my part, I did not sleep. I prayed to Hashem for protection for my King and my family. My worst fears were that Ziba failed to carry out my directions and that the King had no provender. The reality proved far worse than that, for I never conceived of the horrendous and destructive lies Ziba told King David about us earlier that day.

Could Ziba have waited for that day for a long time, since he first came to me in Lo-Debar and brought me back with him to King David? Did I pose such a threat to him? Did his greed extend to the destruction of people and reputations and lives? It seems so. I who never asked anything of him other than what I had asked that day—and that was on behalf of the King—I was his mortal enemy.

Ziba used my idea of supplying the King with goods to his own ends. The train of goods both surprised and pleased the King. Ziba presented them to him as he crossed over the last hill leaving Jerusalem.

"Bathsheba, look at what my son Mephibosheth has done for me!" the King said to Ziba. "Thank him for me, Ziba."

"I would do so, gladly, my King," Ziba said, "but these are not from the son of Jonathan. I brought these out to you."

"Oh?" David said, surprised. "Yes. Mephibosheth knows nothing about it," Ziba lied. "I thought it best to do so since he has betrayed you, also, my Lord."

"Betrayed… me?" the King repeated, bearing another blow to his heart.

"Yes, Lord. He called me to him after you left the city, and he ordered me to bring all of this and all of the money I had in the land's treasury to him in the King's house. He said he was going to use this time of confusion to claim the throne of Israel for the House of Saul!"

This last sentence staggered King David.

"I thought it best, Lord," Ziba repeated, "to bring all of this to you instead, since you are Israel's rightful King."

At the time, no one thought to ask Ziba about the money he claimed I demanded from the land's treasury. The King said nothing for a moment as if he were in deep thought. Finally, David thanked Ziba and told him,

"All the land that you had tended for Mephibosheth is now yours, Ziba. Thank you for your loyalty. I won't forget it."

According to those who were there, and heard every word, Ziba said, "May the King live a long life and live to see a loyal son on the throne of Israel." Bathsheba, near enough to hear the entire conversation, told me much later that she knew in her heart that Ziba spoke lies but that was not the moment to tell the King what she believed.

I confess to you, children, and to Hashem, that to this day I still harbor ill will towards Ziba for the harm he caused the King and the harm he caused our family that day. May Hashem, who has forgiven much, please forgive me for my lack of forgiveness, and I pray that you all may understand.

SIXTEEN

The noises Jordana heard in the house came from the rooms of the King's concubines. David knew and trusted these women. He asked them to have care of the house until he could safely return. If Absalom took Jerusalem, it made no difference. Concubines mattered little to a king who must flee for his life. Having the run of the house, these women took over several of the other rooms, organized the kitchen and laundry, and were as surprised to find us still there as we were to find them. They did provide us with food, but Ariella wanted nothing to do with them, so she would send Jordana and Sheera for our food daily. For my part, I could eat nothing and slept little. Most of the time, I looked towards the eastern mount where the King's train had gone, hoping and praying for his swift return. I did journey to the Tent of Agreement one day to pray, and I found that the high priests and the Ark were there, having been ordered by the King to stay in God's city. The priests had little to say to me, but they allowed me to pray in the outer court. Ariella began to chide me because I refused to eat or bathe or shave or groom my hair. "You will scare Michah," she pleaded, and what she meant was that I scared her. But I told her that my actions mirrored my heart, for I was in mourning for the loss of the King. "At least, drink something, my husband," so I did that at least.

Two days later, we heard great shouting, and at first my heart leapt at the thought that the King had returned home at last, but Sheera ran in from outside and yelled "Absalom's coming!" and my heart sank. True, soon enough the son of David could be seen outside the window, dismounting with fifty or so armed men and many more thronging the street outside the king's house. "Oh, Hashem! Please let him not have killed his father!" I prayed quietly. He entered the house to great shouts from his retinue of "Long live Absalom of Israel! Long live King Absalom!" that caused my heart and head to droop even more. The men made their way through the rooms, grabbing this or that ornament or decoration for a prize, laughing loudly, yelling even louder, with the pleasure men take in the moment of plunder. Each yell caused Ariella to pull Michah closer to herself and the girls huddled behind her. A few times, I saw her make the sign of luck when one man or another would yell.

Soon, one unceremoniously ran into our rooms and stopped short when he saw our little group. It was a soldier of the King's that I knew from the supper table, a Benjaminite, who had rough manners and a crude tongue. Another man came in behind him, one I did not know, and the first man turned and said, "Nothing for us here; he's a cripple," and they left laughing. We all stood still for a moment until Michah said, "Mother, you're squeezing me," and she released her grip on his waist. We all let out a sigh of relief. For some time, we continued to hear the yelling and laughing and looting as ewers were overturned and chairs upended. Soon, we heard the concubines screaming and squealing, and then we heard running on the rooftops. We learned later that Absalom made a large display of taking his father's concubines in front of his friends as a sign that he had truly also taken his father's throne.

Rather than give praise to Hashem, as David might have done, Absalom decided to hold a crude and disgusting "sacrifice" befitting a crude and disgusting man. Jordana and Sheera stared at the ceiling, mouths open, as they heard the cries of the women, until Ariella asked them to help her in cleaning the rooms that had been cleaned already twice earlier that day only to occupy their minds and hands. Michah, again sensing the tension of our situation, stayed close to me but with his head downward. I never showed much affection towards you, my son, but you know that, by Hashem, I love you. You may remember that I touched your shoulder several times that day to reassure you that all would be well. It was as much I knew to do. I am truly sorry if you were not comforted.

Late on the next day, after the inglorious ceremony on the roof and continued debauchery overnight, Absalom, who had only spoken to me in passing in all our years in court, scratched at the outside of our room. At least he had that common courtesy.

"Son of Jonathan," he said, as I came towards the door. "I wish a word with you."

My mind played through the answers I would give him to any number of possible questions. I wanted to remain calm and not display any fear without angering him. After all, he literally held our lives in his hands. "Yes?" I said, adding no title or name to the reply. If he took that as an affront, he gave no indication of it. He looked at me strangely until I realized he looked at my matted, filthy hair and my dirty clothing and feet. He paused for a moment and narrowed his eyes. I thought at the time that perhaps he was deciding if my short answer should be taken as an affront to the position he felt he held at the moment.

"You were the guest of my father here," he began, suddenly returning to the reason for his visit, "but not a guest of mine. Can you and your family be out of the house tomorrow?" His tone was not angry but was matter of fact. Again, to his credit, he could have sent a servant to order us out or simply have us thrown out with no explanation. Or he could simply have put us to the sword.

"I need these rooms," he said by way of explanation. "I ask you myself because of the kindness you showed my sister some time ago."

In all the events of recent days, I had forgotten my night visit to see Tamar. I tried to think quickly, but my words came weakly and with the slight stutter I suffer when frightened. "W-w-we can be out before the Sabbath," I said, thinking that we would have four days to prepare and move, "and we can go to the lands your father gave to me."

He thought a second, nodded, and said, "Before the Sabbath, then. Make it so. I don't care where you go. Take only what is yours."

This last affront I could not abide, and it emboldened me. In a clear tone, I answered, "I would never think of taking what was not, Absalom."

He strode out without a reply. I doubt he even heard what I said—much less what I meant. And, other than seeing him from our windows ride off to chase his father a day later, that short interaction was the last I spoke to or saw Absalom.

SEVENTEEN

Thinking about my encounter with Absalom, it dawned on me that my visit to Tamar months before, if known about by others, could be seen as my having been in league with the rebels against King David, even if my motives for seeing her were good ones. Indeed, we later discovered that one of Ziba's servants had been the shadow Mordecai saw following us, and that servant reported to his master, who then eventually used that episode as proof to King David that I was complicit in the plot against him. I made the mistake of telling my fears to Ariella, who pulled at her hair in fright. At that moment, neither side wanted us, and perhaps King David at least wanted us dead. Worse than those fears, my children, was the fear that he perhaps thought I had betrayed his kindnesses.

The official records tell of the story of Absalom's advisors and how he came to choose the path he did. Of course, Hashem's hand can be seen clearly in this tale, as in all things, which proves that our worries are often unfounded if Hashem is the Good Shepherd who knows best. Absalom made frightful errors of tactics, I am told. Forces loyal to King David, though vastly outnumbered, fought for his name and out of love for him. My servant and friend, Mordecai, loyal to both King and Hashem, even took part in the great battle, he with one hand and years from the training ground. He received a wound from an arrow that scraped his thigh, which he showed me later, and it healed into a scar as long as a man's hand. For him, it became a crown of honor. David's great general Joab himself secured the victory with the killing of the prince. While the story in the archives of Absalom getting his hair caught in the tree is not corroborated by those who witnessed the killing of Absalom, it seems that a low-hanging limb did indeed knock the prince from his horse, and that led to his slaying by Joab.

All of this happened as we finished our packing and began to leave the city as we told Absalom we would. We remained ignorant of all the events that seemed to take place on top of each other those days. I had instructed the girls to never go out of our rooms alone while Absalom's men remained, but as we made our way out of the house, knowing that almost all the men had accompanied the prince to battle, I asked Jordana and Sheera to run ahead and see if any animal still remained for us to use. In the courtyard, they found an old man picking through the garbage left by the rebels. Two equally aged donkeys accompanied him. The girls begged him for the animals, saying that their crippled master needed them and, after returning to me for some coins, they had them ready for Ariella and me at the front of the house as we exited. Michah helped Jordana and Sheera tie some of our possessions to the backs of the animals, and Michah helped his mother mount the smaller of the two donkeys. Each of the children carried a large blanket of items.

It was all I could do to manage myself with my crutches. As we made our way out of the city gate, my heart swelled with tears as I thought back to the great joy we shared when King David first called us to his house those several years before. Now, it seemed, we would never see Jerusalem again. Before we could get out of sight of the city below the hill, however, we heard great noises coming from the road before us. I instructed our little group to give way and move down the side slope of the road, thinking we could hide in the shrubs there and see what the commotion meant. As we moved down, my crutches slipped on the grass and I tumbled head over feet into a bank of brush. Ariella threw a leg over to jump off her donkey, and then she and the others slid down the hillside and joined me in the bushes.

From our hiding place, we saw men on mules and on foot come down the road, shouting and singing. We strained to make out what they were saying and singing. Ariella turned to me. "Did…did they say David has won the day?" she asked. We listened again. Sheera—she with the best ears among us—spoke up loudly, "Yes! King David is victorious!"

The King must have sent the men on the road to take the news to Jerusalem. I sent Michah scrambling back up the slope to the road to ask one of these mounted men if the King were coming back to the city. From the bush, I saw the man reach down from his mule and tousle Michah's hair and laugh. Michah then came scooting back down the hillside to us. "Yes, father! The King is coming right behind!" We burst into joyous tears, all five of us. The relief overwhelmed us. Ariella buried her face in her hands in joy and probably some fear. The girls cried openly. I could only weep tears of happiness. "Let us go out to meet him," I told them, and the girls led Ariella up the slope back to the road while Michah shouldered his load and helped me get to my feet, steadying me as we crawled our way upwards. We and the animals continued down the road for only a short distance before we soon saw the outliers of the King's procession as it crested the hill before us.

Unlike the forerunners who were bringing the good news of the victory, these men wore somber expressions. We stayed to the side as they passed us silently. They did not shout and laugh as the others had done; no, these men seemed to be in mourning. They barely noticed us as we passed them. From behind these men, we heard the sound of a train of animals and implements as they banged together in movement and knew that it must be the King himself. I noticed harsh stares from many in the main group as we made our way towards where the King was. One of the men on foot saw us and turned and ran back towards the King as if to warn him. When we reached David, this man stood nearby him, and I was able to recognize him as another of Ziba's servants.

If possible, the King had aged many times in the short days since he fled from Absalom. The gray that had crowned his head had now been conquered by a snowy white in that time. His head remained covered by a veil, still in mourning, it seemed. I found out later that his anguished cries of pain over the death of Absalom turned his victory parade into a funeral procession. Joab, eyewitnesses reported, scolded his King for behaving thusly, saying that if victory had not been given by Hashem, then all of them would be dead—was that better? Joab shamed the King into not shedding more tears, but one could see at a glance that David's heart remained broken for his son.

As we approached, we saw the King's procession had stopped, as if waiting for me to approach. The coterie with him parted and allowed us to come up before David. I saw Bathsheba riding on a mule beside the King, and she gave her niece and me a flat smile when our eyes met. However, my presence before him provoked no visible change in the King's face.

"Mephibosheth," King David said flatly in a voice of an old man.

Throwing down my crutches and falling to my knees, I answered, "My King."

He looked over my head as if the sight of me caused him pain, and the look shot an arrow into my heart. He nodded at nothing as he continued to look beyond me. "Mephibosheth," he repeated. "Why did you stay in Jerusalem when we left?"

The question came more as a true search for information rather than an accusation, so I answered him the only way I knew how. "My King, I wanted nothing more than to go with you. Ziba betrayed me and, I fear, you as well."

At this, Ziba's young servant turned to go back in the train, but David's raised his hand and said, "No. You. Stay." The King's command stopped the young man in his stride "Explain," the King ordered, turning back to me.

"You and your household left so quickly. I knew you had few supplies. I sent Mordecai to fetch a son of Ziba's to prepare a train of goods for you and then to return for us once you were supplied. Ziba himself came, my King, and promised he would do as I asked, but neither he nor any of his house returned for us."

"Bring Mordecai, the son of Joseph," David ordered to some men around him. Soon, Mordecai, using a stick for a crutch, hobbled up to the King, and, upon seeing me, he smiled grimly and nodded. Relieved to see him alive I, too, smiled thinly and nodded, relieved to see that his wound did not seem too serious.

King David asked Mordecai if what I said was true; Mordecai promised the King that I had instructed him to fetch the son of Ziba. David asked if the rest were true. Mordecai hesitated and looked at me. He bit his lower lip in thought, and the King pushed him. "Come, come, is what he says true or not? Answer me."

I could see that Mordecai did not wish to harm me, but he valued honesty and truth above most other virtues. "I cannot say, my King," he answered. "I did not hear what Mephibosheth said to Ziba, so I cannot say in truth. But I do know that Mephibosheth loves you, my Lord."

David turned and looked up at Bathsheba, who nodded slightly to him. It seemed to confirm something in his mind.

Before he could speak, I added, "I have been in mourning, too, my King, for you. Since the day you left, I am as you see me. I have not bathed. I could not eat from worry about you. Sleep, too, has left me."

The King turned back to me. Still not looking directly at me, he said, "Yes, I received the goods. Ziba informed me that they came from his heart, not yours. He claimed you wished to use the situation to restore the House of Saul to the throne of Israel."

From behind me, I heard Ariella gasp, and the sound drew the King's attention. "Are you all well, Mephibosheth?" he asked.

"Now we are, my King," I answered.

He sighed, as if he did not know what to do. "When Ziba told me of your betrayal, and in light of what I supposed was his generosity towards me, I proclaimed that he should receive all the land of your grandfather that I had given you. Now, hearing and seeing you, I think I will give half of it back to you."

"Oh, no, my King," I cried, tears of relief streaming down my face, "Please, do not. Give it all to Ziba! I wish I never had it! My land— my pasture—is seeing you return to your city and your throne. That is enough for me, my Lord. I cannot tell you the joy it brings your servant." With this, I put my face to the dust of the road. Again, who was I, my children, to demand anything of this man who had done so much for me?

David paused, again in thought. Finally, he said, "Get up, Mephibosheth; someone…help him up," he ordered, and two men picked me up from the dust of the road.

My tears, held back by my fear, suddenly turned to the King's face, and he looked at me now. I saw my tears mirrored in his own eyes. "You have answered from a pure and good heat, my son," David said to me, "and I restore all the land to you."

"To see my Lord alive restores me, oh King!" I answered. And he smiled weakly at me through his tears.

EIGHTEEN

E ven though King David returned to his city and his house and his throne, more calamities awaited him. Seeing a vulnerable land with an aging ruler, neighboring nations rose up to pick at the edges of Israel. David grew too old to lead his people in battle, and generals such as Joab waged war in his name. Some years of pestilence and famine awaited, too, before the King died. He who had led such a charmed life well into his middle age found his waning years among the most difficult known to any man.

As for Ziba, David called him to accounts over the falsehoods he told about me. Ziba found himself stripped of any income and responsibility as caretaker of the land; in addition, David confiscated much of the income Ziba had taken from me over time, and there was nothing Ziba could do about it. He died shortly after the King returned, and no one from Jerusalem mourned him, it seemed. Rumors we heard from servants said that he was eaten by worms from the inside. It is no matter to me. These days, I see a son or two of his on occasion, but they are quick to avoid crossing my direct path. I'm told one of Ziba's grandsons recently petitioned King Solomon for restitution of the lost funds, but the wise King would not even give ear to the case. I am certain a grudge from that family remains against me, but I cannot worry about the anger in the heart of another man. Besides, I am too old to care. And I have no needs or even wants that Hashem through King Solomon does not meet.

Bathsheba told me later (for I never broached the subject with the King) that Ziba had indeed used the "evidence" of my visit to Tamar as proof that my loyalty lay with my own selfish ambitions and not with the King. The night after Ziba came to him with the supplies, the King, lying in his tent and with enemies all around him, actually cried to his Queen about my supposed betrayal. This tale stung me deeply; I was amazed that my actions could have been taken for anything but what they were by the King who had done so much for me. The King's feelings also (may Hashem forgive me!) aroused a bit of pride in me that my actions could affect the King so much, until I remind myself that, while the King may have loved me, any love he felt for me actually sprang from his love for my father.

Bathsheba said she felt Ziba thought Absalom would put me to the sword and that Ziba's lies about me would never be found out. "I never doubted, Mephibosheth," she once told me, "and, in his heart, I don't know that the King ever doubted you, either. So many other things happened then that occupied our minds." Perhaps she told me that to comfort me, for I saw his face when we met him on the road, and I saw he felt I had betrayed him. I thanked her for the gift of the story in any case. I also found out from her that Machir, my father-in-law and former benefactor from Lo-Debar, assisted the King during his short exile. David inquired about me, and Machir showed surprise that David would even express any interest in me, thus confirming, in my mind at least, that he felt no real understanding of or love for me. Yet, Machir was loyal to King David, so I am grateful as well to him for that.

In addition, I learned later that Ziba told the King that Mordecai, too, felt no loyalty to David, pointing out that Mordecai made the trip to Hebron with the conspirators. However, Mordecai's bravery on the battle field—even with one arm—proved that this tale was a lie as well. As for us, David asked Mordecai's family to take Ziba's place as the caretaker of my ancestral lands, and I gladly increased my friend's share of the profit annually. Thus, we again settled into a routine for a time at the King's house.

Something died in David when Joab killed the young man Absalom. David spoke more and more of walking humbly before Hashem, and I think he was reminded of the pride in himself reflected in the actions of his son. No, the King was not the same man who slapped his knee in laughter those years ago when first meeting me.

Over the coming months and years, joy came to us in gifts great and small, such as seeing the King once again play his lyre on the rooftop, seeing him smile at dinner, or the blessed, happy marriage after some years of your mother Sheera to Michah and the start of their own family. Jordana, may Hashem bless her, remained devoted to Ariella and never married; she who cared for my dear wife until her death also found joy in nursing and helping to raise you, my grandsons, to young manhood. I still see her on the rare occasion. She has become a midwife and is, in this sense, at least, the mother of many children.

So, yes; Hashem is good.

While the betrayal of Absalom burned, the betrayal of Israel left an even deeper wound of a kind in King David. In his declining years, he searched for ways to reunite with his beloved people, but no real reconciliation never occurred until after his death, when the outpouring of love and affection for him came from all corners of the land. Shame on those who withheld their hearts from Hashem's anointed during his later lifetime!

Meanwhile, I saw daily reminders of David's love for my father's family. We relied on the protection of the King and of Hashem—as we shall always do, my children.

NINETEEN

I knew that Ziba's not unexpected betrayal still stabbed Ariella to her core, as did any evil action by man, and it wounded her because evil did not exist within her. Harm her, and she would forgive and perhaps even understand. Harm those she loved, and you would wound her mortally. Such love and protection towards family runs strong among the women of our tribe. While Ziba never laid as much as a finger on my wife, I will go to my own death believing that his actions gravely injured her. Her weak heart became much weaker as a result.

The town of Gibeon lies to the north and somewhat to the east of Jerusalem, and people not of Israel live there to this day. In an effort to purge the land of these unbelievers, my grandfather, King Saul, years ago burned much of it and destroyed crops and many lives. Perhaps it would have been better if King Saul had wiped the place from the earth, sowing salt in the fields so none could live there forever. There is no indication that this desire to harm the Gibeonites came from any place other than Saul's own perverse heart.

Some years after King David's return from the Absalom exile, a severe drought brought starvation across the land. For three years, almost no rain fell on Israel. This caused King David to inquire with Hashem as to the reasons for the lack of rain. The answer David received from Nathan pointed to my grandfather's evil actions against the Gibeonites as the cause of the famine that afflicted the land. So, in an effort to appease Hashem and to heal the land, the King sent to Gibeon to see what recompense the people of the town required to end the drought. At the time, we gave the thing little attention, thinking that a sacrifice to Hashem or perhaps some tribute to the city would suffice, but were happy that at last we knew what the cause of the famine to be.

I had learned long ago at court to not take references to my grandfather to heart. As I have said, I never knew the man. And his actions, while having an effect on me, I did not have to answer for before Hashem. Many was the time an old soldier of David's would say something unkind about King Saul and then look to me and apologize, red-faced, having forgotten I was present. I would assure the man that no offense was taken and remind him that Hashem anoints the King—then and now—and we must accept His choice.

The unfortunate coincidence was that, during the time King David appealed to Gibeon, Mordechai and I had gone to our land. The journey was one of the few times I had actually seen the land that had been the object of such contention for so long. I wished to accomplish three things with the trip. First, I wanted to take the time to see the burial site of my ancestors, for who knew when I or Ariella would be taken by Hashem? I wanted to know what would be required when the family needed the place. Also, Mordechai and I wished to see for ourselves what damage the drought had wrought to the impending harvest. Lastly, we wished to offer sacrifices to Hashem for our own issues with the famine. We planned to be gone for over a month. Thus, we did not know that the Gibeonites asked of King David that seven male descendants of Saul be given to them as blood recompense for the wrong done them so long ago.

My children, the crown of Israel or of any nation cannot rest on the head that cannot make difficult choices that will benefit the people. Hashem, as I have said, knew that such choices could not have been and cannot be made by me. My father, bless him, had the mettle to make them. The current King, Solomon, has it. And King David, who rests with his fathers now, he had it as well. David used lots and selected two of my uncles and five of my cousins and gave them to the Gibeonites in order to save his people from the famine. As I said, it is the choice a king must make.

The second unhappy coincidence came in the fact that I shared a name with one of my uncles given to the city of Gibeon. So, when the King's herald read out the names of those selected, it had occurred to no one to make a distinction between my uncle and myself. I found out about the decree when my now almost fully grown son Michah came riding a mule to find me and Mordechai on the land. We hurried back to find that Ariella had taken to her bed, severely ill—it was her weak heart again—when she heard the names on the herald's decree. I found out later that Bathsheba thought the same, and the thought had moved her to tears.

Dear children, I do not blame King David for this. His hands are innocent. It was by his seeking Hashem that the famine ended and the Gibeonite curse was lifted from the land. No, he bears no guilt in the matter. My dear wife, Hashem bless her, she did blame him. In what remained of her life, she never said she forgave King David for not making the distinction. The shock of hearing her husband's name on the list of the soon dead struck such fear in her that she died a few weeks later, never rising from her bed. What injury Ziba's betrayal had begun, the shock of hearing my name as one of the soon to be dead dealt her the final blow. I pray Hashem gave her peace in her heart before she died, peace towards the King that gave us so much. My regret to this day is that I was not there to reassure her when the names were read. Perhaps even my presence could not have averted the shock, but I tell myself it could have done so. Hashem comforts me with the thought that He knows our hearts and directs our paths; part of my trust in Him is that I must accept that in all things.

The event and deaths of Saul's seven descendants touched others profoundly, as well. Rizpah, my grandfather's much-aged concubine, the mother and grandmother of these men, became touched in her head by her sons' deaths. Yes, my children, as you probably know, after her sons and grandsons were put to the sword by the Gibeonites, Rizpah took it upon herself to protect their bodies from corruption for almost a year. During all that time, she shielded her dead from wind and storm, shooing away flies and vultures as the bodies remained where they were slain, immediately outside the gate and wall of the town of Gibeon. When a proper time had passed, King David ordered that the bodies be taken and buried. Rizpah had to be forcibly removed from their care by strong men, so crazed she had become. She never became restored in her head, and she died soon afterward, also of a broken heart.

King David used the burial of Saul's descendants as a time of renewal among the people. He sent a servant and summoned me to him shortly after Ariella's death, one of the few times he did summon me to his presence after his return from exile during the Absalom rebellion. He summoned me so that he could ask my opinion.

"Mephibosheth, would it hurt you if we buried your family together in your family tomb at Zela?" he asked.

"No, my Lord, not at all," I answered, still not quite sure what he requested.

"I mean your father and grandfather as well," he said.

I squinted at him and shook my head, still not fully understanding what he asked.

"Sit down, my son," he said. I sat on a chair that Ira the Jairite produced in front of the King's chair. "I have something to tell you. As you know, when your father and grandfather died at Mt. Gilboa, their bodies were displayed publically by the Philistines in Beth-shan."

I knew.

"I have received the bones of these two mighty men of Israel from the men of Jabesh-Gilead. Good men there took the bones out of the square in Beth-shan out of respect, and they have kept them all these years. No one knew for sure who had the bones," David explained, "but we have found them."

From somewhere, and without either of us realizing it at first, tears began to flow in David's eyes and in mine.

The King continued: "I want to do honor to your father and grandfather, who have never been recognized by Israel, and I want to honor the dead of their family, those who died so that Israel might be spared by famine. Would you, as the remaining head of the family, allow it?"

I dried my eyes with my sleeve. I had not thought of myself as the head of anything other than myself, Ariella, and Michah—but she was dead, and Michah had his own household.

"If the King wills it, it is my duty to obey," I said. It could be that the King wanted to pay respects to Ariella as well, and including my opinion in the matter was his way of paying honor to her through me. I took it as such.

"No, my son," David said, "I'm not commanding you to do this. You have nothing to obey but your own desire in this thing."

I thought about that a moment. "Yes, yes," I said suddenly, changing my mind once I had been given opportunity to do so, "I give leave to do this thing." David seemed pleased by my response. He also knew that such a task would occupy my mind, and for that, too, I am grateful to him.

Having only recently opened the tomb of my great-grandfather Kish to bury my beloved Ariella, I knew the size of the tomb and what would be needed to bring in the nine other remains. King David would not hear of me paying the expenses of travel and preparation, but I insisted on paying for the sacrifices, reminding the King of his own words when he had purchased the threshing floor where Hashem's temple, built by Solomon, now stands:

"I will not offer Hashem that which costs me nothing."

The large memorial feast-meal after the remains were laid in the tomb was somber but also healing; Israel sent men from all tribes to Benjamin to honor not only those seven but also the memory of King Saul and his son, my father Jonathan. Men who I thought had never noticed me came by where I sat and touched my arm or said a blessing over me as if they knew me well, and some told me stories of my father and grandfather that even the King had not told me before. Many also paid great respect to Ariella, which surprised me. I never realized so many people knew her and honored her loyalty to me and to the King.

In all the days of my life, that day was the closest I came in my lifetime of being treated like a prince of Israel. And I pray I am not being proud or impious or disrespectful of the dead to say that I did not find the experience totally disagreeable. I will say no more of this matter, other than to honor the King that sought to honor my family with this request.

Hashem was satisfied. The drought ended immediately.

We almost danced in the glorious rain of Hashem's mercy.

TWENTY

If the family wishes to know more about the great deeds of King David of Israel, let it seek the official records in the archives in which I now sit to write this. His actions were many and mighty; Israel, as King Solomon rules it today, remains the great people it is because of David. I say this knowing that King Solomon agrees with me, for he has told me exactly so himself.

King David ruled in Jerusalem three decades. His watch over his people—his sheep—and his love for each of them, cannot be measured. As I have said, he aroused great jealousy because he himself loved so passionately. A lion he was, even in death. Several more wars waited for David. The King insisted on going out for some of them, as his strength would allow. He would be in the camp, in the tent or around the camp fire during the battle, but at least the soldiers could see that their King shared their experience of the field. That meant a great deal to them.

Once a Philistine, rumored to be a descendant of the mighty giant Goliath, swore to take vengeance against David by entering the camp and killing him. The man was cut down by David's mighty man Abishai, but even the thought of losing the King in battle scared the soldiers around him. The decision was made—and not by King David—that he would not be allowed near the battlefield any more. As he left the battlefield for the last time, the King was said to have quoted from one of his early songs, a song that was written when David sought to get away from my grandfather, King Saul. Part of that song says:

I will call upon the Lord,
Who is worthy to be praised,
And I will be saved from my enemies!

King David returned to his house in Jerusalem and rarely left after that. Much of the remainder of his time was spent thinking and talking about the building of the temple of Hashem.

In short time, David slept more than he was awake. Doctors did not know what to do. Then, he did not even leave his bed. The sickness that took him by the hand of Hashem stalked him slowly until he could no longer sit upright much at all. A fever came and went in him. He had enough of his mind, however, to ask that his bed be moved into the throne room so that he could be nearer those he knew and loved and so that he could hear the court musicians play his favorite compositions. But even his own soothing songs could not keep him from dropping more and more away from life.

By this time, Bathsheba remained the only wife that could ever be seen in proximity to the King. Many had died over the years (including my aunt), but most of his wives merely stayed in their own houses and contented themselves with their children or grandchildren. In collaboration with David's chief steward, Ira the Jairite, Bathsheba ran the day-to-day operation of the house. No real evening meal had been served in some time; the cooks prepared a mid-afternoon meal that most took in the throne room simply to be near the King; small groups of twos and threes even sat in the room, cross-legged, to eat their meal near their beloved David. It was as close to the battle camp ground as David could get at that moment, and his men brought it to him.

The deathbed had commenced.

Here I, too, would sit near the dying David as the life ebbed from him over the days. He spoke little during those times, but suddenly one day, quite clearly, he looked at me having waked from a deep sleep and spoke, quietly but quite clearly.

"It's cold, Jonathan; it's so cold."

The king lay shivering on his bed, so from my chair next to him I reached and pulled the fur cover up and around his neck until it cushioned the gray mass of hair of the old man. The covers stirred the air around his aged body, and a wave of the death smell wafted up to my nostrils from the king. I sucked in my breath through my teeth in an effort to not have the stench in my nostrils. He struggled to open his eyes wider and focus on my face as I did so, and then, his eyes narrowing, realized that I was not his long-dead friend but was, instead, merely the crippled son. He nodded acknowledgement, and I attempted to soothe him by saying, "My King, you were only dreaming. See, it is I, Mephibosheth."

David heard the whispers of his men and the servants across the room and through the doorway. "They think I'm crazy," he said lowly, turning his head towards the hushed tones. "They're up to something," he added, looking back at my face.

"They only want what's best for you, King David," I said, sitting back in my chair.

"Why am I so cold?" he asked no one in particular, slipping back into the dream-state. "The desert," he said, "In the desert it got this cold at night." Then, remembering where he was to a degree, his reddened eyes widened, and he added, "But that was a long time ago, wasn't it?"

"Yes, my King," I said, "Almost fifty years ago, sir."

Ira the Jairite interrupted our conversation. "My Lord and King," the servant began and waited for some recognition by David. The king used to pride himself in knowing every servant, every slave, every man of his court—and most of their families, too. He had prided himself on knowing them. It was the mark of good king, he told me once, to know your people well—as his Lord knew him. But David barely registered any recognition of a man he had known well and practically seen daily for some time.

Seeing that the King didn't respond, Ira continued. "Allow me to present to you your servant girl, Abishag. She will help you stay warm." The servant turned with his fleshy, untanned outstretched arm and, from behind him, a small, dark, and lovely maiden with large, downcast eyes came forward. She wore only a simple but elegant robe and her brown feet were naked. The girl bowed in reverence before the king. As I struggled into my crutches and moved away from the bedside, Ira helped the girl disrobe, and she slid into the bed beside David. Her young, vibrant skin must have felt almost hot to his own. I turned slowly to see if she would give him comfort, and saw that she, too, was shaking, but not from cold.

"Thank you, my child," I heard David say to her softly and soothingly, as she moved closer to him in the great bed. He feebly stroked her brown hair, pulling it back from her face. "She is lovely," David said aloud, but her warmth acted as a great blanket to the king and he quickly slept in her embrace.

Ira smiled and, waving both hands like a farm woman shooing chicks, quietly motioned for all of us to leave the throne room and let the king sleep in peace with the girl.

TWENTY-ONE

What we did not know was that in that same moment, when the King lay shivering with Abishag, Prince Adonijah, David's next in line to the throne, took several select members of Army of Israel on maneuvers in the plains west of Jerusalem. With him rode General Joab. Joab, we learned later, had come to love Adonijah, to think of him almost as a son. After all, the boy had always been a soldier; he had grown up behind the saddle of almost every one of the Thirty Heroes. In Joab's eyes, Adonijah would make a good king for a people constantly at war with surrounding enemies.

Joab had known, before most everyone else—certainly before David—that Ammon would never be king. Ammon's passions always got the better of him, and a man who cannot master his own passions cannot be the master of others. On the other hand, Joab had often said that Absalom could have been great as a leader and a soldier. "Who knows," he would often say, out of earshot of King David, "what could have been?"

And within David's hearing, not long before the king took to his deathbed, Joab had asked David, "Who is left besides Adonijah? Surely not that weakling son of Bathsheba!"

David did not reply to this, so Joab felt he had permission to continue, "It must be Adonijah! He remains the only sensible choice."

And now, Joab showed the people where his own loyalties lay. In his eyes, perhaps, David would be dead at any time—was dead, for all practical purposes. In his eyes, it was time for the new king and he, Joab, was the kingmaker.

While Adonijah and Joab took the army through its paces, David showed some signs of rejuvenation. He had even regained enough strength to sit up on the side of the bed. The mood of the entire city lifted with the king's stirring. Heman and Jeduthun, the king's musicians, played a selection from one of David's early compositions in the corner of the room as I made my way towards the bed for a visit. Ira had told me it would be a good day to see him as long as I did not tire him too much. The tune they played sounded joyful and happy, and the music reflected the feeling of all in the room.

Abishag was on her knees on the bed behind the king, and she used a stiff brush to work the knots out of David's tousled gray strands. It seemed she brushed and pulled in time to the music. Care for him had been turned over to her almost exclusively, and David did not seem to mind. Abishag's initial fear over being in the presence of the king seemed to have been diluted and turned into true concern and love. Ira gave her all the credit for the improvement in the king's state, even if it were only a temporary improvement.

The smile that brightened the king's face on my approach told me he recognized me, and I returned his smile. "Sit... there," he said, still laboring to catch a full breath, and nodding to a nearby chair. I did so, and the king nodded again, saying with his head and face what he could not with words. He was glad to see me, and I acknowledged that great gift.

"My family remembers you in our prayers, oh, King," I told him.

"And… mine… you," he said between brush strokes.

"I am happy to Hashem that you look so well, sir," I said, adding, with a smile only for him, "He lets you catch your breath."

"You… remember…," he gasped, as Abishag continued to brush in time. "…Good!"

TWENTY-TWO

Later in the week, Bathsheba and I took some time to ourselves and sat on the palace roof in the evening. It had long ago ceased to be seen as anything untoward about our friendship since the household knew we both loved the King and that she had become truly as a sister to me over the years. As we sat in silence, looking over the rooftops, Prince Solomon came up the stairway and made his path over to where we sat.

"Any news of the King?" he asked after he had greeted us.

Bathsheba sighed and beckoned her son to sit beside her on the couch. She turned to me for confirmation and said, "He is much the same, don't you think, Mephibosheth?"

I nodded. "The same, yes, but the trajectory is downward, Solomon," I said, probably in too much of a matter-of-fact manner.

"Ira the Jairite found a Shunamite girl to keep him warm and to take care of him," Bathsheba added.

"Does that hurt you, mother?" Solomon asked, touching her hand as it set next to his. All three of us looked at Bathsheba's hand. Between the wrinkles, one could still see signs of great beauty having once been there.

"Solomon, my son," Bathsheba smiled, looking at me, "Your father and I have been together too long and have been through too much to be anything but secure in our love." She turned to her son and said, "No, it does not hurt me. I only want the King to be happy...for the time he has left."

"You know," she said, looking behind me across the city, "It was here, on this rooftop, that your father and I had our first private moment."

"Yes, so you have said many times," Solomon said, but he did not sound put out. "Nathan reminds me to the story often, except he tells it as if it were a fable from long ago that happened to different people, not to you and the King."

Bathsheba's gaze fell to her feet. "Oh, but it was a long time ago, my son. And your father was a different man then. I wish you could have seen the King in those days, Solomon. Ask Mephibosheth. David's smile could melt your heart. He had a great lover then, you know."

Solomon's face frowned. "I never knew that; who was she?"

Bathsheba smiled again, and I saw where she was going with her story. "His lover was Israel. The people were in love with him and he with them. He could get the people to do anything he desired, and they would have done anything he asked. That was all before..."

"...before Absalom." Solomon finished.

"Before everything," I added.

She turned to her son and grasped both his hands in hers. "But that is what a king is supposed to do, my son. The true love of his life should be his people." Mother and son looked at each other for a long time, and none of us spoke.

In that moment of silence, a great, deep conversation occurred between queen and prince. I left them there to finish the discussion and excused myself to go check on the King. As I made my way downstairs, my thoughts were torn between the conversation on the roof and the events in the room where David lay dying. As I slowly descended the stairs, I prayed, "Hashem is my shepherd… please, give King David pastures of tender grass in his last days."

When I arrived in the throne room, the King was waking from a sleep. "My Lord," Abishag whispered into David's ear as she shook his shoulder gently, "Wake. You are only dreaming; all will be well."

As I moved closer, I could see that David had been crying in his sleep. Now awakened, he allowed the girl to dry his eyes with a cloth. He sat up and coughed, and Abishag wiped the sputum from his mouth.

He then saw me sitting next to him and said, quietly but with great effort, "I dreamt of your father. In my dream, we were out in a field shooting our bows and laughing. Suddenly, his bow broke its string. I offered to restring it, but I could not. He looked at me with such sadness—it broke my heart."

I did not know what to say, as my own eyes began filling with tears. It was Abishag who answered for us all.

"If he is a friend then he should understand," she offered.

"Oh, yes!" the King said, turning to her, "this friend understood everything. He was the finest man I ever knew."

"What happened to him?" she asked, innocently.

"Ah!" I exclaimed, eager to tell the story myself for the first time— and forgetting my manners by addressing her directly since this girl was not of our family.

At that moment, Ira, the chief steward, approached and interrupted us. Abishag quickly gathered her cloths and brushes and water pan and retreated to another room. Ira grinned broadly at the King. "Hashem be praised! My King is looking better today!" Ira's pink, bald head leaned down, and he assisted David in sitting on the bedside. Even the effort of sitting upright tired the old king.

"Yes... better," David managed to say.

Ira offered, "Can I get the King some food—I trust he is hungry?"

David responded, "Yes... a bit. Not too... much, Ira. And, Ira... thank you for the... young woman."

"It was nothing, my King," Ira straightened, then bowed and left to get the food. During the time he was gone, I did most of the talking to the King, not wanting him to tire himself with speech. I told him about my grandsons, told him some palace gossip (which made him laugh quietly), and was about tell him about spending time with Bathsheba and Solomon when Ira returned with a bowl of steaming soup and some simple brown bread.

"Perfect," David said, as Ira pulled a small table up to the sitting King. Abishag returned and fed the old man his meal, carefully wiping his mouth and beard with a cloth when the spoon missed its mark or a coughing spell brought more sputum from his throat.

The King thus occupied, Ira leaned down to my ear and whispered, "Do not speak to him of Solomon, nor of Adonijah. Let him be, I beg you." A bit shocked by Ira's insistence, I had not given the rivalry between the two sons for David's throne much thought.

"Yes," I whispered in response, and it made sense. A dying man does not need the extra burden of a potential battle for his crown while it still rested, however precariously, on his own head.

"I shall let you eat in peace, my King," I told David, rising on my sticks.

"See me... later," he said between bites.

"I shall do so, sir," I answered.

Ira followed me out. "My apologies, Mephibosheth," he began, but I shook my head.

"It is I who should have been more careful, Ira," I said. "You are correct; he does not need to be reminded that his successor has not been clarified."

"Those were my thoughts as well," Ira agreed.

While talk of the impending clash between Solomon and Adonijah never found voice in the throne room, elsewhere in the palace the topic dominated. For example, the Prophet Nathan, who said his evening prayers from the second-story balcony of the palace, in a voice that thundered over the courtyard, even used one evening to devote the prayer to the situation.

"God of Abraham, Isaac, and Israel, hear me! I am your servant Nathan." His booming voice stirred to flight an evening flock of pigeons over the King's house. "David, Your servant, is dying. Oh, Lord, God of Israel, give him comfort. May his kingdom be secure! Even now, men plan to harm Your people. Defeat them, Lord! Bring justice to Your people in the name of David of Bethlehem. You have chosen Jedidiah to rule; make it so! Give me strength and wisdom and power to be Your instrument in this and all things and to help Your dying King. To Hashem be glory forever!" The cries of the swirling pigeons answered him as his words echoed off the palace walls. Everyone had heard. Not as many believed it would turn out as Nathan had prayed for it to. In fact, other, powerful men allied themselves against Solomon and for Adonijah.

It was one of these days that Ahio, the servant of Abiathar, one of David's high priests, came to the palace with a secret. Ahio had been present during a meeting between Joab and Abiathar about the succession. According to the report, Abiathar was enjoying some wine and some figs when Ahio announced a visitor. "General Joab to see you, my Lord," he told the high priest.

"Yes, I think I can spare some time out of my busy day to see an old friend; show him in, Ahio."

"Don't bother," Joab had said, already in the room. "And Ahio," Joab added, without turning to the servant, "Show yourself out, please."

But Ahio listened to the conversation from the doorway. According to several who heard it directly, the man told the story well; how Joab helped himself to the high priest's wine and figs, how he asked Abiathar for help. Abiathar had said, "Let me guess; you've found a new girl and want to marry her? You've found an older girl and want help getting rid of the husband? Oh, I know; you want to be king of Israel?"

"You aren't far off on the last one," Joab answered. "I have a deal for you."

Abiathar answered, "I haven't kicked you out of my house yet; I'm listening."

"What do you want more than anything?" Joab asked. "What has been galling you for decades? Yes; I promise if you help me, you will be the only high priest in Israel."

Now, my children, in those days, King David kept two high priests; this Abiathar and one Zadok. Joab now promised to remove Zadok if Abiathar would support the succession of Adonijah.

"Joab, I'm afraid your history of violence testifies that whatever price you want me to pay for this honor, it will be too high for me to pay. I'd rather be owner of half a priesthood than owner of none."

"Listen, you idiot!" Joab shouted, standing up and spitting fig remnants, "This is your chance!" Abiathar put a finger to his lips, and Joab sat back down and leaned in towards the priest.

"Our chance," Joab hissed.

Ahio eavesdropped on the rest of the conversation and then ran to the palace to tell the prophet Nathan all he had learned. According to Ahio, the two conspirators arranged a meeting with Prince Adonijah at Joab's house. As Abiathar's servant, Ahio accompanied his master to the meeting, although his heart belonged to King David and to Hashem. All of this he reported to those loyal to David. Rather than a quiet, private planning meeting, Adonijah had turned the journey to Joab's house into a festival. He hired five squadrons of armed men to precede him, and he drove an expensive chariot with white horses. Crowds heard of the approaching parade and soon thronged the streets in that part of the city; they crowned his head with fresh yellow flowers and men as well as women reached through the press to try to touch his chariot as it rode through Jerusalem's streets.

Somewhere in the back of the crowd began a cry of "Long live King Adonijah!" and the handsome prince in the chariot only turned to acknowledge it and waved, so the crowd forgot the cry and responded with a great roaring cheer. In many ways, Adonijah could be more trouble than even Absalom had been. He had the same charm, the same good looks as his brother without the complete lack of morals Absalom had. A half-good man is more difficult to read than a purely evil one.

At Joab's house in the northwest sector of the city, Abiathar listened to the growing tumult as the crowd and their hero drew closer. "I thought we were going to have a quiet meeting with the boy," the priest said to Joab, "and instead, you've turned it into a victory parade!"

Joab responded with a laugh as the procession entered his courtyard. "Perhaps this meeting is not needed after all, Abiathar," Joab said. "The people think he is king already."

TWENTY-THREE

Nathan took the information Ahio gave him and went straight to Bathsheba. She had been around court long enough to know when gossip carried any threat to it or not. This time, she saw that Nathan's face betrayed serious concern.

"Man of God, next to Mephibosheth, you are my oldest friend here," she told Nathan. "You have been the King's greatest advisor. I have been hearing rumors, and I fear for the King. If you know something, please speak freely. I wish to speak to the King today. Please keep nothing from me."

She later told me that Nathan's old, yellow eyes narrowed as they looked at her. "I held out little promise for you when the King risked his kingdom for you," he began, "but I must admit that you have been the most faithful of all the King's wives to him and to my God."

Nathan paused to let that compliment sink in. He continued, "Yes. There is something you should know and something the King should know. And it should come from you." And he then relayed to her the plot to take the kingdom away from Solomon.

"Know this—that God has chosen Jedidiah to be the next king of Israel," Nathan reminded her. "The King, too, knows this in his heart of hearts but, because he is dying, he forgets the promise he made to you and to your son before God. If King David is not reminded of this promise, and soon, the lives of you and your son may not be worth much."

Nathan's words caused Bathsheba to draw her breath in sharply. She knew what she had to do. At that moment, a servant came to the door of the Queen's rooms to announce a visitor—the head of the King's bodyguard, Benaniah. He begged apologies of Nathan and Bathsheba, but they dismissed his manners quickly.

"Do not stand on niceties," Nathan ordered. "What news?"

Benaniah reported that Joab had made the rounds of the soldiers and had quietly told the King's personal bodyguard, both the day and the night watch, that they were to request a leave of absence from their duties for the next few days. The King would have been left unguarded! All but a small number did not even consider the request—thank Hashem! Joab overreached, it seems; he should have known that the King's own bodyguard would not have left the dying man completely unattended for even personal reasons. Benaniah then confirmed what Ahio had relayed, that the conspiracy was to make Adonijah king while David was too weak to stop it—and without David's blessing as well. Benaniah even said that preparations were being made at that hour for Adonijah's anointing by Abiathar.

Benaniah's son, Jehoiada, had been one of David's closest advisors, but he had spent most of his time at his farm in Kabzeel since the King took to bed. Jehoiada sent word to his father that the King must declare once and for all an heir of his own choosing, now, because the army as a whole would not hold out long if they could be convinced that David was not capable of choosing an heir. It was David's choice to make, he said; the true soldiers of David did not desire a king of Joab's and Abiathar's choosing. David must act before Adonijah had the throne well in hand. Sooner, not later—later might be too late.

Yet, the King lay dying. Bathsheba had no time to waste. She now felt confident that those around the King, at least, remained a true and loyal core.

So, she sent word to Ira the Jairite that she wished to speak to the King as soon as the King could see her. Ira sent back word to wait for a time, since he had an audience with Haggith, the mother of Adonijah, at that moment. "More of Joab's maneuverings, no doubt," Benaniah remarked to Bathsheba and Nathan with pursed lips. Bathsheba waited in an empty room adjoining the throne room, and she saw when Haggith left the King. The two wives of King David looked wordlessly at each other, and Haggith paused as if to speak, but then continued on down the hall. David had been good at keeping his wives separate, Bathsheba thought, so the two women knew each other only by sight and reputation, but they had never spoken. Bathsheba asked me once if I knew what she was like, but I did not. Perhaps she assumed that I had some connection to others outside of the court that she did not, but I assured her that she was the only one of David's wives with whom I ever spoke outside of formal introductions at festivals or special events.

Obviously, Haggith possessed no great beauty—certainly she was no Bathsheba—which means that Adonijah received his handsomeness from his father. Haggith's marriage to King David had been one of convenience, since her father ruled a neighboring kingdom. David acquired land from her father with the marriage. No love existed there, Bathsheba felt sure, but she knew of David's loyalty, loyalty that exhibited itself often to a fault and that never turned away loyalty, even in his wives. The scowl Haggith wore on her face as she left the throne room told Bathsheba that, whatever it was she requested of King David, he did not grant it. Ira the Jairite appeared at the door and diverted her attention.

"The King will see you now, my lady."

TWENTY-FOUR

According to those who were there, the sun shone brightly upon the ephod of Abiathar, the high priest, and burst into hundreds of sparkling reflections that danced across Zoheleth Rock. Despite having to let his priestly robe out more and more every year, Abiathar still made a striking and imposing figure in his priestly costume.

As the twelve trumpets blasted, one for each tribe of Israel, the animals prepared for sacrifice were brought forward. Abiathar had gone over the ceremony and rituals with Adonijah earlier. Someone remarked, inappropriately, it seems, that Solomon would not have the stomach to perform the sacrifices required in the ceremony, but Adonijah shrugged and said he really did not know since Nathan had taken over the rearing of Solomon—his brother remained a mystery to him. In any case, Joab said, soldiers like Adonijah grew up used to seeing blood, no doubt.

Adonijah raised the sharp curved knife high over the bleating, struggling first sheep and, with a powerful downward stroke, thrust the blade deep into the animal's throat. But he struck badly; blood splattered across the front of the Prince's new robe, and some even splashed on the ephod of Abiathar. Whispers began among the men assembled that the struggling of the animal and the poor strike of Adonijah made for an ill omen at the start of any reign. But then, the trumpets sounded again, drowning out the cries of the dying animal and any negative whispers.

"The King is dead! Long live King Adonijah!" Joab's toothless mouth roared when the trumpets' sounds reverberated away across the hillsides, and the men left the hillock for the banquet table. For Adonijah, a young man I barely knew, it must have seemed easy. He was a pawn of Joab and then, it seems, Abiathar as well. It came out later that Abiathar, at the last moment, had recommended that the ceremony crowning Adonijah king should wait at least until David was properly dead. After all, how long could it be until he was? That way there could be no one to dispute the claim of an eldest heir. But Joab's concerns stemmed from his belief that David was being manipulated by Nathan, Zadok, and Bathsheba.

So, in answer to Abiathar's fears, Joab—the man who fought great battles at David's side and in David's name—said, "David is already dead; he's been "dead" for years, and the army will follow me where I tell it to go." In this, he reminded me of my relative Abner, who had propped up my uncle, the idiot Ishbosheth, after my grandfather died all those years ago. Abner, the kingmaker, whom Joab himself had killed. Abner, he who taught Joab nothing.

Those celebrating the crowning of Adonijah that day are said to have consumed more wine in that one sitting than all of Israel usually consumes in a year. Perhaps they were trying to convince themselves through the grape that what they did that day was right. Drinkers, of whom I am not one, call it Wine Courage.

TWENTY-FIVE

While the Adonijah faction celebrated their coup, Nathan and Solomon talked on the hill that lay to the east of the city.

"You know that the Lord our God chose you to be king of Israel when you were born, do you not?" Nathan asked. "All the signs at that time confirmed it."

"Yes, Nathan," Solomon answered his tutor. "I know. So you have always said."

"Yet, you say that if Adonijah wants the throne, you will let him take it from you?" Nathan could not understand the young man. Solomon had been an unusual person since childhood, Nathan said. He always answered questions with other questions, and this tried the patience of the old prophet. Solomon did so, again, now.

"Perhaps Hashem means for Adonijah to be king for this moment; did God say that I would be king when my father died, or did He say that it would simply happen one day in the future?"

"Jedidiah," Nathan said, exasperated, as if talking to an obstinate child, "you are Hashem's chosen one. You are your father's chosen one. Why are you trying to ignore these facts and try my patience?"

Solomon thought a moment. Then he said, "You always said that the Lord's will cannot be stopped. If the Lord God wants me to be king, then I shall be. There is nothing you or I or my father or Joab or even my brother can do to stop this. My question is whether or not the time for me to be king is now. Hashem's time is not our time."

Nathan let out a breath of relief. "Good! You have spoken well."

The pair walked to the crest of the hill that allowed them to look over the brook into the city. From their vantage point, they could clearly make out the white-washed house of the King that stood above the other buildings of the town like a citadel.

"Do you trust that the Lord has chosen me to be his instrument to you?" Nathan asked.

Solomon did not answer right away.

The old prophet persisted. "Well? Do you?"

The young prince nodded and looked towards the King's house.

"Then hear me," Nathan instructed. "God wants you to be king. He wants you to be king in this moment. In fact, he wants you to be king while your father the King is alive to see it."

"Yes," Solomon said with finality, nodding. "Yes, you are right. Then tell me, man of God, what do I need to do now?"

A large smile broke across the wizened face of the prophet. "You yourself have said it," Nathan answered, spreading his arms wide. "There is nothing you need to do; it is in God's hands!"

And so, after blessing the young man with both hands, Nathan headed towards the King's house while Solomon made his way to the Tabernacle of God for prayer.

TWENTY-SIX

King David always asked Bathsheba, "What can I do for you?" He still asked that question when she appeared before him that day. Ira, who witnessed the encounter, said that Bathsheba's eyes travelled from David to Abishag and back, and that the King noticed. "You can speak before her," David said.

The King's meeting with Haggith had tired him even if it did not last long. Bathsheba said that when it came her turn to see him his breathing came rapidly and shallow, like a man trying to stay above water. Yet, even in his distress, he saw her pain.

"My dear... what troubles you... so?" he asked.

Bathsheba could not keep her emotions stored for so long and, seeing her husband's compassion for her hurt, she burst into tears and threw herself down in front of the King's bed.

"Why?" she asked softly, looking up at David through her hair, "Why did you name Adonijah as your heir? You made a promise to me—you swore that our son Solomon would be king!" Bathsheba composed herself somewhat and added, "Then... today... Adonijah was crowned king of Israel!"

David pitched forward on his bed with the shock of the news, phlegmy coughs wracking the old man's frame. "Ad... Adonijah?" he asked breathlessly.

"Yes," she answered softly, rising to her knees, bowing her head, and blotting her watery eyes with the edge of her fine robe. "He performed the sacrifices this morning in the presence of and with the blessing of Abiathar, the high priest, and Joab, the general of your army."

"Joab... was there... too?" David began coughing again, this time as if he had been run through with a spear. Abishag lovingly and deftly wiped his mouth and beard of the spittle.

Bathsheba, her eyes still glistening, rose and stood with her head bowed. "They invited the officers of your bodyguard and the army as well. As we speak, they are feasting Israel's new king. Please," Bathsheba begged, as her tears began again, "please tell me that you did not give your blessing to this usurper. Our lives are in danger if this is so; yours, mine, Solomon's. Are you so ill that you have forgotten your promise? Are you still my husband? My beloved..."

Her voice trailed off into tears.

The King began crying also.

Behind him, Abishag wiped a tear of her own away and wished at that moment to be anywhere but there. But the King turned to her and said, "Help me up." With the girl's support, David stood, summoning the last of his strength. Standing shakily above his wife, his tears dripping down upon her head, his breathing even more labored, he said, "Haggith wanted... my blessing on Adonijah... and I did not know... why she asked. But... it makes sense... now."

He reached a trembling hand and touched the top of Bathsheba's head in blessing. "My dear... one," he said, shakily stroking her gray-streaked hair. "My own... dear... one."

Bathsheba raised her head and looked with glistening eyes at her husband. His hand fell rather than moved from her hair to her cheek, and he wiped a tear with the back of a finger. She managed a feeble smile at his touch.

Abishag, a simple but good girl who told me much of this later, realized that years of love and knowledge travelled between their moistened eyes. The King began to sit, and he thanked Abishag as she helped him sit back on the bed.

From the doorway and across the room, Ira began to announce, "Nathan the proph..." but he was cut off by Nathan's hand and loud command of "Out of my way!"

"Yes!" he yelled as he approached David's bed, "it's all true. Today your son Adonijah has proclaimed himself king of Israel."

David kept his eyes on Bathsheba's tear-streaked face. She searched his in return and, satisfied that he was in his right mind, whispered, "All Israel watches you now. Show them that the Lion of Judah is still king!" She rose, bowed before her husband, and left the room.

The King sat back on his bed, and Abishag propped him up with pillows. "Maybe Adonijah thinks... it is... his time," David said.

Bowing slightly before the King, Nathan answered, "My King, you've never had to say "no" to that boy before; you must say "no" to him now."

"You are right... man of... God," David said, looking the prophet in the eye. Summoning his strength with a full but labored breath, he continued, "This smacks of Joab... I can smell his scent on this as if he were a dog... marking his territory."

Nathan showed a largely toothless grin.

"Yes," the old King said, nodding, "there is still... some sense left... in me yet." David reached behind and beckoned to Abishag for his cup. She gave it him, and he drank, spilling much of it on beard and bed.

"Not much sense left," David repeated after the drink, "but some." He closed his eyes for a moment as if to gather himself.

The prophet used that pause to give the King more information. "They have assembled a rather strong faction, my King. Besides Joab and Abiathar, some of the army group leaders have sided with Adonijah."

"Any of the Heroes?" David asked, opening his eyes wide and looking up from the cup.

"Not one, my Lord. But if there is no alternative, they would be disloyal to not follow Adonijah. He is, after all, the eldest remaining heir."

"And Abiathar with them? I never... should have appointed two... priests. One is always... plotting against... the other," David said.

"Is it possible you gave Adonijah your blessing?" Nathan asked.

"No..." David said, casting a questioning look first at Ira and then back at Abishag.

Ira confirmed it. "No, my Lord; you gave the young man no audience, even."

"Send in... my wife." David ordered, handing the cup back to Abishag and sitting back in the bed.

There was no question in Ira's mind which wife the King meant.

TWENTY-SEVEN

Alone in the outer court of the Tent of Agreement, Solomon prayed.

"Lord my God; You have always been kind to my father, David. He has lived and walked in ways that are good and right in Your sight. You have always shown him great kindness. And You have always blessed me, even before I came out of my mother's womb. I know You will allow me to become king after my father. But, Lord, I am afraid! I am like a little boy! You have taught me the things I need to know to live right by giving me Your servant, Nathan, to guide me. But I do not know how to be a king. I do not have wisdom!"

The curtains of the tent flapped in a sudden, strong gust of wind.

"I need the guidance of Nathan inside me; I need the strength of my father inside me; I need Your mercy and wisdom inside me in order to rule and judge the people rightly."

As he uttered these words, Solomon told me, years later, he began to feel a calmness run through him. "The ceremony of my crowning and anointing by Zadok that followed that day was only a formality," he explained. "God had already made me king. I knew it in my heart."

What Solomon did not realize was that at that same hour his father the King issued one of his final decrees. Shavsha, the scribe, came to my rooms and asked if I would start making my way to the throne room as quickly as I could. When I asked as to why my presence was needed, all he did was call over his shoulder as he turned back towards the door was, "Just hurry!" My first thought was that the King was dead, but that news would not have come to me by way of Shavsha.

By the time I had made my way to the King, I saw that he was sitting on the side of the bed. Great care had been taken to groom David's beard and dress him in an expensive but comfortable robe; a small diadem sat far back on his head to insure it would stay in place on the weak old man. Facing him stood Nathan, Bathsheba, Ira, Zadok the priest, and Benaniah the general. Several lesser servants hovered at the fringes of this group, including Abishag. Behind all of them stood the bodyguard. Shavsha sat nearby at a table, furiously scribbling the list of witnesses to the event. Obviously, the occasion concerned the succession.

King David saw me come in—my servant assisting me—and he nodded a welcome and motioned that I was to stand up next to Nathan on the far left of the first group towards the bottom of the bed. The crowd waited patiently as I made my way to my assigned position.

"The Lord my God gave us His promise… of protection for the people," David began when I had found my place. "This promise has always been before my eyes. In the same way, I now… renew the promise I made several years ago to many of you here today. Upon my word," he said, stretching out his hands in blessing, pausing to get his breath because the effort was draining him, "I promise to these assembled here today… and in the presence and power… of the Lord, God of Israel, that my son… Solomon will be the next king after me."

Tears again wet Bathsheba's face, but the tears ran down her cheeks past a large smile. She dropped to her knees before the King. "Long live King David!" she exclaimed. Nathan stood next to me, nodding approvingly.

The King had spoken.

Zadok, the High Priest, found Solomon in the Tent of the Agreement as Nathan said he would. Several remarked that a king should be found in prayer often, and the event carried the power of a being a good omen.

"My son," Zadok said to the Prince, "come! We need to hurry. Today you shall be king of Israel." Solomon followed the high priest out of the tent. There, a caravan of Nathan, Benaniah, several members of the bodyguard, and the King's mule greeted him. When Solomon mounted the animal, Benaniah, at the head of the small column, turned in his saddle and yelled, "To Gihon!"

The worshippers and priests surrounding the Tent of the Agreement realized what was happening when they saw Solomon mount the King's mule, and they began to cluster around him with shouts of good wishes and blessings. A huge cheer went up from the growing crowd as the group made its way towards the Gihon Spring.

As soon as the sacrifices had been made (and all reported that Solomon struck the animals well, unlike his brother), from the surrounding trees and up from the hills came several heavily armed soldiers. Zadok's old eyes grew wide with apprehension. Had Joab sent a death squad to eliminate the rivals? He then heard Benaniah laugh. And then Ammizabad, one of Benaniah's sons who was one of the heavily armed men, said, "King Solomon! It is my honor to present the Thirty Heroes—your personal bodyguard!"

TWENTY-EIGHT

Adonijah's coronation feast was winding down when the noise of Solomon's crowning as king reached the celebrants. Jonathan, one of Abiathar's sons, ran to the banquet hall and broke the news to the revelers. It was reported that most had been in a drunken stupor and that Adonijah had two young girls on his lap, each one taking turns feeding him grapes.

Seeing Jonathan, Abiathar is said to have waved the young man in the room and asked, "Is King David dead?"

Jonathan simply said, "No. The news is not good for you. David has made Solomon king this day."

It was at this point that Adonijah stood, sending the grape girls flying off his lap. Adonijah demanded of Jonathan how this was possible,

Jonathan shrugged. "Zadok anointed him. Nathan, Benaniah, and the bodyguard witnessed it at the Gihon Spring."

At this news, two army officers got up from the table and, gathering a third, less sober colleague by an arm each, hurried out.

"You're too late," Jonathan called after them, "because the army is with Solomon."

Joab's face became blood red, and he began pulling his beard in a succession of rapid strokes as if this would make the news go away."

"The people are with him, too," Jonathan added. "They brought Solomon back to the palace and put him on David's throne. Then the servants helped the old man himself get down and bow before King Solomon."

"Don't you dare call him that!" Adonijah said, threateningly. He then ran from the room.

Abiathar fell back in his chair, clutching at his heart. He yelled at Joab, "What do we do now, you old fool?"

At the opposite end of the long banquet table, Joab leaned forward to speak.

He vomited instead.

The outpouring of devotion and love that the people of Jerusalem showed towards Solomon amazed many in the court. Citizens who had known David for years brought expensive gifts for the young king and placed them all around the throne. A line of well-wishers ran out of the throne room and even out of the palace into the streets.

From the King's bed, David and Bathsheba, sitting on the end of the bed, both watched and smiled tired smiles. Yet, David still mustered the strength to rest a weary hand on his wife's knee.

Some of the presenters even offered their daughters or sisters to Solomon as suitable wives. He politely refused and even added the right compliments to them so that they left pleased and not offended.

"He will be great," David said to Bathsheba. She spoke little, but she seemed to glow in the moment as she looked from father to son and back again.

It was in the midst of these events that Ammizabad, another of Benaniah's sons, ran in to the throne room and breathlessly announced, "Adonijah is holding the horns!" A buzz ran through the room. So the usurper sought sanctuary and a reprieve by entering the altar room and grabbing the altar horns. Out of instinct, several court members turned to David to see what his reaction would be to this. But David's eyes looked to Solomon, and that caused these courtiers' eyes to follow David's. Soon, when the buzz died out somewhat, Solomon spoke, and the crowd was stilled.

Firmly but gently, King Solomon said, "If my brother shows that he is a good man, and a loyal subject, then I promise by Hashem that no harm will come to him."

The crowd in the throne room applauded approvingly. Shavsha quickly wrote what King Solomon said and noted that the sentence marked the new king's first decree. Yet, Solomon had not finished.

"Ammizabad," he continued, "Take some men from your squadron, and bring my brother to me." Ammizabad quickly pointed to several men, and they began to leave. The King stopped him. "Ammizabad," he said sharply, causing the soldier to stop at attention, "Do not harm him. Is that clear?"

"Yes, my King." Ammizabad turned, bowed, and left, followed by his detachment. The room buzzed again, this time in agreement over the way the young king handled himself and commanded respect.

At this point, David lay back on the bed and closed his eyes; now, he could rest.

TWENTY-NINE

Aservant later reported that Joab seemed to not be able to pack his things quickly enough. He even was willing to leave the seven silver goblets that he'd captured in the wars against the Philistines and which he prized so much. That was the moment when Nathan entered his house and yelled, "Joab, son of Zeruiah! Stand fast!" Joab froze in place while putting some clothes in a sack. Nathan continued, laughing as he said, "So! The mighty general, the Defender of Israel, runs away at the last moment! Do you not know you cannot run from Hashem?"

Joab turned as quickly as his hangover would let him. "You son of a whore! You're behind this! Deny it!"

Nathan then stopped smiling. "Joab, you have won great victories for Israel and for your king. Do you for even one moment think that all you have done was by your own power? Are you so old that you have forgotten that the Lord God of Israel guided your hand and your sword?"

As he spoke, according to what I heard Nathan tell others, one could see Joab sag lower and lower, his face dropping with each pronouncement. Nathan continued his admonishment.

"You! David's own general and kinsman! You who lived by the sword shall surely die by it. When did your heart turn from using your sword for God's purposes to your own ends?" At the end, apparently, Joab listened to all of this with a resignation, as it Nathan only spoke that which the general's heart had already told him.

"Joab, of all people in Israel," Nathan said, in conclusion, "Yes, you should know that what we do matters little compared to all that is wrought by God's will. True, it was your sword, but it was God's hand! Ask for his mercy Joab. It is all that remains for you!"

Nathan departed without another word as Joab finally sank until he sat on the floor. Nathan was able to hear as the servant reminded him. "Hurry, General! We must leave!"

"Shut up, you fool!" Joab answered, his voice ragged and raspy, and added to no one but himself, "It's over."

The prophet later told me that his own heart sang songs of praise to Hashem as he made his way back to the King's house.

THIRTY

With the three-day coronation celebration of the new King Solomon ending, the thoughts of all in the court turned again to the dying David. Perhaps he felt that his work had been completed; he had seen the kingdom finally peaceful and had lived to see the crown of Israel rest on the head of a son of Hashem's choosing and his approval. His favorite wife was pleased. It was the end of a great, brilliant reign. Yes, he had wished to build the great temple to Hashem, but that task would fall to a man of peace, Solomon, not a man of war like David.

There were only a few more important things that David felt he must do before death, and he called his son, the new king, to his side one morning in the harvest time. Most of those close to David remained at his side. There was nothing now that could not be said in front of the household, so Solomon and Bathsheba, Nathan, Ira, and I sat in a half-circle around the side of the bed of David as he instructed his son one final time.

"Trust Hashem above all else. If you do, you will do well all your days."

"Yes, father," Solomon said, patting his hand. "I know."

David smiled weakly. "Don't talk. Listen."

We all grinned for a moment through our tears. David was the only one who could speak to the King this way.

"Yes, sir," Solomon said, with his own smile to his mother.

"Take care with your sons. Choose your replacement wisely. You see what can happen if you do not."

Solomon nodded but didn't speak.

"Joab…" David began, but his voice cut off.

"What about Joab?" Solomon asked.

"Do not let him go in peace. He lived by the sword; let him die by it."

We exchanged surprised glances between us, but Nathan interjected, "I told him as much myself."

David nodded then continued. "You know best, Solomon. And Shimei, the son of Gera. Him, also, do not spare."

"Yes, father."

"The sons of Barzillai, they were kind to me when I ran from Absalom. They will be loyal to you. Bring them here. Let them eat at your table."

"Yes, sir."

The effort spent at speaking this much wore David out. He seemed to have more to say. He hadn't the strength or breath to say it. All he did was to catch Solomon's eye and motion with his own eyes towards me as I sat near the foot of the bed.

Solomon looked down at me and then back to David. "Do not worry, my father. He is like my uncle whom I love."

David nodded slightly. Solomon had understood. So did I.

The tears flowed freely among all of us as King David, the Lion of Judah, the great and mighty warrior of God, closed his eyes and slept with his fathers.

It would be the last time all of us would be with David.

I miss him, greatly, still.

THIRTY-ONE

When Abishag had been given care of King David, she had felt that God had given her a special gift; of all the women in Israel, it had fallen to her to provide comfort for the King in his last days. It was a badge of honor she said she would carry for life. Yet, before he died, the steady stream of advisors, servants and—sometimes—children and relatives that paraded before David's bed daily barely noticed or acknowledged the young woman who stood nearby to wait upon him. This did not bother Abishag; in fact, the only thing that bothered her was that David never asked her for her name. He always and only called her, "my child."

Once, when she was trying to untangle the mane of gray hair on the old man's head, one particularly difficult twisted knot pulled out with great effort, and David groaned.

"Oh, my King!" she apologized, "are you hurt?"

"No, my child," he wheezed, "I have felt... much worse."

Still, it hurt her that she caused him any pain. She told me all this as she made her preparations to move to a small room in the house after David's death. Ira would be sure to see that, as the King's last bed partner, she would have a place in the house as long as she desired it. Her devotion and love for David seemed so true and genuine. He was her King. She was his servant. That was it. It was simple to her because she was a simple woman.

So it came as a great surprise when news came that Adonijah had taken her as a wife. Shades of Absalom flew past my eyes. Technically, Abishag was not even a concubine of David's, so why Adonijah would see taking her as somehow making any possible claim to the throne any stronger remains a mystery to us all. Solomon had pardoned his older brother when the men dragged him, screaming like a woman, away from the horns of the altar and into Solomon's presence. In front of the entire court, Solomon calmly and respectfully told Adonijah to dry his tears, calm himself, and listen. Then he proceeded to give his brother these instructions:

"You will live peaceably with me and with all men. You will respect our traditions and both of our mothers. If you agree with these conditions, you will live a long and honorable life as my brother and in the service of Hashem and the people."

Adonijah stopped his tears of fear, only replying with a sniffle or two as the wonder of the mercy Solomon offered him began to sink in. But his brother wasn't finished.

"If you refuse to acknowledge Hashem's choice of me as King of Israel, I will give you two options. First, you may leave this land, never to return. Or, if you so choose, you will be put to the sword."

Adonijah stifled a fearful cry. For one such as he who had grown up around the army, who had known battle, it surprised me that such a man as Adonijah would show such fear before others, much less before women.

Solomon finished by saying, "If you live honorably and as a worthy man before Hashem, you will live, and you will live in peace. Do you understand?"

Adonijah said, loudly, through a nose filled with phlegm and tears, "Yes!"

"Go in peace to your house, my brother," Solomon said. With that, the men who had brought him in then escorted Adonijah out.

Now, with King David dead and buried and still mourned, Adonijah had decided to make trouble for the new King by marrying the woman—the girl, really—who had cared for David in his waning days. The official record says that Adonijah asked for Abishag through Bathsheba. That is not quite correct. He, like his older brother Ammon, took her for himself without asking. This I know for the girl herself told me so. And Bathsheba became involved because Adonijah came to her to ask forgiveness of Solomon rather than permission. Bathsheba, being the kind person she was and, feeling that Solomon was secure in his reign, presented Adonijah's request before the new king.

"Absolutely not," was the short answer Solomon gave her, and he resolved that Adonijah had broken his pledge to live in peace and prove himself a worthy person by taking Abishag—for whatever reason. The reason did not matter to Solomon; the fact that she was taken without asking is what troubled him.

We heard later that day that Benaiah, the son of Jehoiada, went to Adonijah's house and sliced his neck with a knife. The man was buried with his father, David, without any fanfare at all. He was mourned by none. As far as I know, Abishag was with no other man after that. She died some years ago of a cough. I felt sorry for her.

The death of Adonijah seemed to open the season of harvest on David's and Solomon's enemies. Joab knew he was next, and he went to the tent of agreement and grabbed the horns as had his protégé, Adonijah. It did him no good. When he was ordered to come out by the King, Joab refused.

"Let me die where I am. Solomon doesn't have the courage to kill me here," Joab reportedly said. Benaiah, acting on Solomon's orders, struck him down there, saying, "You're wrong, again, Joab. This is from Solomon."

In issuing the death order, Solomon said, "Joab shed innocent blood without the leave of David or Hashem. Strike him down, bury him, and release me and my family from the guilt of the blood he has shed."

It was discovered later that Adonijah and Joab had a scroll on which they listed their enemies and those they would kill when power was finally theirs. Of course, Solomon and Bathsheba, as well as Nathan and Zadok, were on the list. Near the bottom of that list was my name, too. I thanked Hashem that He had spared me once again, and I was glad that Ariella wasn't alive to feel that fear even after the fact.

Lest some think that King Solomon refused mercy, hear how he dealt with Abiathar. He sent word to the priest, saying, "You deserve death, but I will spare you. Go to your house. Never leave your land. I spare you because you carried the Ark of the Lord for my father and shared his affliction during wars against his enemies." Still, Solomon stripped Abiathar of any priestly responsibility. Solomon insured he would have only one high priest at a time. The old priest died shortly after he was exiled to his lands, falling off his chair at dinner, dead before he hit the floor.

The people felt that both decisions—to strike Joab and to spare Abiathar—were the proper course to take, just and wise before Hashem.

As for Shimei, he, too, received mercy to a degree. He was ordered to his land as well, but he broke that order after a time. Solomon's man Benaiah took care of him as well. For such service to the King, Benaiah, as you know, was made the General of the Army in Joab's place.

Thus, Solomon secured his kingdom, eliminating all possible threats.

With the kingdom at peace for the first time in decades, the Great and Wise Solomon turned his attentions to building the Temple of Hashem.

THIRTY-TWO

King Hiram of Tyre has proved to be one of Solomon's greatest allies during his reign. The Tyrennians are known throughout the world as great sailors, and King Hiram helped King Solomon establish a navy that would bring trade goods to Israel from lands so far away that we did not know they even existed—spices, precious metals and stones, and even fabrics previously unseen in our lands.

I have seen the sea only one time, from a mountaintop, at a distance. Yet, I have spoken to men who have sailed from the city of Etzion-Geber on the Red Sea with the Tyrennians, and they report strange things they have witnessed. I know nothing of sailing or of these distant lands, only rumors about such incredible things as blue men with three eyes and many arms. It is difficult to believe but, with Hashem, I suppose all things are possible. We did receive a monkey at court one day, and he caused much excitement among all present, but he proved to be a filthy, unclean animal. I think one of the King's soldiers took him home.

The wood that is produced by Hiram's lands, from the tall cedar trees, Solomon used in the construction of Hashem's temple. Also, the trade goods, the gold, ivory, and other precious stones were utilized. Trade routes that united both Egypt and the Tigris were safely established under Solomon's reign, bringing more money and power and land to Israel than ever before.

Yes, Israel has prospered under Solomon's rule.

The building of Hashem's house was only one of the changes Solomon brought to David's city. New streets, defensive walls, storehouses, government buildings, and trading market spaces all came to be in a matter of years. Most spectacularly among these secular buildings was the palace of King Solomon, in which I now live.

After seven long years of construction on Mt. Moriah, all of Israel and representatives from several peoples around us came to witness the dedication of Hashem's temple that Solomon built. The sun shone brightly, even though it was harvest time, around the New Year. The burnished bronze of the columns that framed the massive doors to the building burned with the reflection of the sun, and all the limestone on the exterior made the edifice something to behold. I praise Hashem for allowing me to live to see the day.

For the following eight days of the celebration, the priests offered so many animals to Hashem that the number cannot be told or determined. Flames and smoke from the fires carried the wafting smell of roasting meat up over the city and upwards to Hashem as a pleasing sacrifice from the altar. Then, in the middle of the festivities, a large procession of priests, singers, players, and officials from all twelve tribes, led by Solomon himself, brought the Ark of the Agreement to its permanent home. Oh, but it was glorious! The King honored Michah with participation in the parade as a representative from our tribe of Benjamin, while I was able to watch the wonderful procession from my window. No more would the Ark of God have a temporary home as it did for almost five hundred years.

Inside the building, the Ark was brought first into the outer court, then to the inner court with prayers, songs, and supplications. Finally, the holy box rested in the Holy of Holies, where one man, representing all of us, meets Hashem once a year. The Ark has had quite a journey from the desert with Moses, through the years of the wandering, into the land of promise with Joshua and Caleb, through the terrible years of the judges and then to be captured by the infidels only to be returned and, finally, brought home by David and Solomon to Hashem's beautiful house.

Praise be to Hashem!

When the massive doors opened to allow the Ark in, the inlaid gold of the inside of the doors and the gold on the floor and walls sparkled like a thousand suns radiating throughout the city. The people gasped loudly when their eyes were momentarily blinded by the beauty the building revealed in the sunlight. This use of gold made the building so costly but, as Solomon says (and his father, said, too), "Nothing is too good for Hashem."

Tens of thousands of baskets of wheat and hundreds of thousands of gallons of olive oil are shipped to Hiram's lands every year to help cover the cost of the building of Hashem's temple. The trade that Israel made with the world gave the King's treasury more than ample stores to meet this payment and more. The soldiers in the army now fight with the greatest weapons; war chariots and especially trained archers with iron arrow heads stand ready to defend and fight for Israel at a moment's notice. The farmers use metal scythes to harvest their grain. Copper mines and iron mines now dot the land in the hilly areas of Israel.

Yes, the Israel of Saul and David is no more. Solomon has made Israel the envy of the world. Bathsheba, she who remembered as much as I and even more, remarked such to me shortly before she joined David in death.

"We are of the old breed, my brother," she said one evening as we dined in her rooms. I rarely go downstairs or dine at the King's table anymore; the meals are too rich for me and the table too loud and too crowded. These days, usually, I have my meals as well as tablets and scrolls and work brought to me. My eyes are fading, so I often have to have a young scribe read the tablets and scrolls to me. Bathsheba's loveliness had not faded much; like a fine wine, she grew better with age. The beauty she kept in her eyes and heart still shone wonderfully to everyone she met, every person upon whom her smile rested.

"I am pleased with Solomon, but King David would not recognize his city today. I'm not sure I can find my way about it even now," she said with a chuckle.

"It is beautiful, but you are correct," I agreed. "It is too much change for me."

"Do you remember how I would try to make you laugh when you were a child?" she asked as we ended our meal. "You were such a serious boy. You're even a serious old man."

"I don't think I had much to laugh at, Bathsheba," I replied as we ate our grapes and goat cheese. I didn't mean the remark to hurt, but she furrowed her gray brows in response.

I attempted to soften the moment. "Am I an old man, sister?" I teased her, adding a smile.

She beamed back at me. "I don't think I've seen you smile maybe a handful of times in the years I have known you, my brother. Could it be that you are finding joy at last?"

"Perhaps, my sister, perhaps. I am getting weaker, this I know."

"Ah, but the joy of the Lord is our strength, Mephibosheth!" she said, brightening.

I looked down at the ring I still wore on my finger, the ring David had given me the day I arrived in the village of Jerusalem all those years before. The ring stayed there as a constant reminder of the joy at the providence of Hashem through King David and now through King Solomon.

I looked up at Bathsheba and nodded. "Yes, of course; you're right."

"I fear for the next generation, though" Bathsheba said, changing the subject slightly. "They don't know the Lord as we did."

She was right to an extent. With the death of Nathan—the old prophet had died some years before—there is no one to speak as the oracles of Hashem any longer.

"Yet, King Solomon is wise, my sister," I reminded her. "Have you read his Scroll of Sayings? He has recorded all that Nathan—and you—have taught him. Surely his sons and daughters will read his wise counsel."

"Perhaps," she said, wistfully. "Perhaps my grandchildren will listen to Solomon's wise words. Israel needs a king whose heart belongs to Hashem. No matter how grand we become as a city and a people, we still need a good shepherd over the people."

"Hashem will provide," we both said, together, and we smiled at each other.

CODA

Everyone has heard of the story of King Solomon and the two women who brought a baby before him. The official record indeed sketches the bones of the tale in strokes of truth. What the record omits is that Solomon, in reaching his decision as to which mother would get the child, recalled another king in another time who, when faced with a choice over which person held truth and goodness in his heart from Hashem, decided on the one who was willing to give it all up for something greater than himself or the object of his desire.

I know this for I was there and, when he said this, the King smiled at me and nodded. Tears for our beloved fathers flowed between us in that moment. For this, I owe King Solomon a great debt, because he honored my love for his father in this decision.

The lands of my ancestor Saul, over which Ziba lied about me to King David to obtain, the land that David restored to me fully, remained in our family until recently. I decided to sell a good portion of it to Mordechai's son and give the money received from the land to the building of Hashem's temple. I came to realize that it was never

Saul's, nor Ziba's, nor even mine. It had been Hashem's land and Hashem's money all along.

Our family's burial sites I did not and will never sell; they will, as I have said, receive my own broken body soon enough. The remaining small plots of the usable land, my children, I give to your father Michah to do as he sees fit. Not that we have need; Hashem through the generosity of King Solomon has seen to it that our family will be cared for.

From my windows in Solomon's fine palace of great value, I can see the beautiful new Temple of Hashem built by King Solomon, although my eyesight grows dim. I remember the threshing floor that King David bought for the purpose. Tradition tells us that it was also the site of our Father Abraham's sacrifice of his son, Isaac. Thus, it has been holy ground since we have been a people. And now, the great building shines in the sun, reflecting the beauty of Hashem. Yes, it is a fine and wonderful building; it would probably make King David uncomfortable if it were a dwelling for a person, but even it would not be fine enough for David's God. Nothing could ever be. When it came to giving Hashem what was His, David spared nothing, not even his own heart.

So, too, King Solomon. He is a man of refinery, yet he has great wisdom and the whole world knows it. And he has been kind to me as was his father before him, and I have already said more about his parents in this scroll than I should.

Ariella remains the greatest blessing Hashem gave me—she and you, my children. That little girl who stumbled and crippled me did me much more good than she ever did harm. Her thoughts, immediately after she had the news of the deaths of my father and grandfather, were to protect me. What love! What devotion! She did not think of herself. That was your mother, children. She bore guilt her entire life for what happened to me, but should not have, and I told her so, often. Her heart was Hashem's. Like King David always said, "Hashem does not want sacrifices; Hashem wants our hearts bowed before Him." Ariella's heart was humble before her God.

What if I had grown up as other boys, grown up and been whole and fearless and not lame and fearful? Would I have grown to be angry and ambitious and thirsty for the throne of Israel and sought my vengeance against David and our enemies? Probably. And that would have seen my destruction, my destruction and that of my family. So, it was a good thing that I became as I am.

I have come to believe that Hashem, as in all things, knows what is best for me. As King David said, Hashem is my good shepherd.

And I have seen much in my lifetime and traveled farther than anyone in my family ever thought I would despite wars, fears, hiding, famines, plagues and these dead legs. Men who have wished me dead a thousand times are rotting in their tombs. As King David sang to me, so it is; Hashem served me a feast-dinner right in front of my enemies my whole life. Thanks for it all belong to Hashem!

Yes, by the mercy of Hashem, my Great Shepherd, I am still here in my pasture of tender grass.

EPILOGUE

Michah, the son of Mephibosheth, the son of Jonathan, the son of Saul, who was a king in Israel;

This record was discovered after my father's death. It was among his things in his rooms in the palace of the great King Solomon of Israel. As with my father's and King Solomon's wishes, this record is to be sealed and placed in the archives of the king. Let it be a record of the goodness of Hashem to all who may read or hear it.

My father died in his seventy-first year, following my mother who had died many years earlier. She, who was his cousin, nurse, crippler, and then wife, loved him as a daughter of Hashem should love her husband. To me, he never spoke of the injury he suffered at her hands. The fact that they loved each other so despite this terrible shared tragedy is a testimony to the power of Hashem to heal our hearts if not our bodies.

May it always be so with our children.

To the Director of the Archives of the Great and Wise King Solomon, King of Israel.

AUTHOR'S NOTES

We know so little about Mephibosheth. The story interests me because *his* story of redemption is much like *our* story of redemption.

The Bible narrative becomes much more (rightly so) concerned with David and his lineage after Saul's reign ends. The mentions of Jonathan's son in the text only serve to highlight David's nature and struggles. David indeed brought Mephibosheth to him in Jerusalem. I like to think that it pleased King David to be able to look down his dinner table and see the son of his bosom companion there.

The Bible tells us that the David-Jonathan relationship was, with the possible exception of the one with Bathsheba, the strongest and most important of David's life. David even marries Jonathan's sister, Michal, in hopes that he will have a child that shares his and Jonathan's blood.

When Michal proves to be barren (after chastising David for dancing in front of the Ark of the Covenant), Mephibosheth becomes the closest thing David ever gets to that dream. Perhaps the young man resembled his father enough that the similarity thrilled David's soul. So great was his love for Jonathan.

Perhaps that helps explain why David so sharply feels the sting of what he is led to believe is Mephibosheth's betrayal. For David, it is the final, cruel cut, when he believes Mephibosheth might be using the Absalom rebellion for his own gain. To be fair, perhaps Ziba must have felt his own betrayal, too, by David or, perhaps, betrayal by Mephibosheth. After all, Ziba took care of (and possibly gained some wealth through) Saul's lands for some time after Saul's death—only to see the lands and possible income be taken away by Mephibosheth's arrival on the scene.

Ziba's report to David about the reasons for Mephibosheth's decision to remain in Jerusalem restores the lands to Ziba completely. Does Ziba get them back permanently after Mephibosheth relinquishes any claim to the land? Or does David restore all the land to Mephibosheth? Or, as the text suggests, does it remain divided?

Scholars have certainly been divided over the Ziba/Mephibosheth issue. Nothing in II Samuel indicates directly that the chronicler feels that one or the other tells lies to David. The narrative sort of simply… ends.

The best clue, however, from my perspective, comes to us in the form of Solomon's much later decision regarding the two women who bring the baby to him and ask him to choose which one is the true mother. The comparison between the two situations includes a description of one of each pair of claimants who is willing to give up what he/she wants for the Greater Good.

While Mephibosheth never receives a verbal (textual) forgiveness from David for not leaving Jerusalem, the young man's "correct" attitude can be reflected by Solomon's giving of the baby to the woman who would rather see the child live with the other woman than have the baby split in two. Division of the land and division of the baby can be seen as the same. I simply assume David restored all the lands to Mephibosheth. Ziba disappears from the narrative at that point.

There are several other things I wish to explain about my writing of this story. First of all, I chose to use the name "Hashem" for God throughout the text. It means, literally, "The Name", and it is used when a person is not using the name "God" in a directly religious sense. I like that name better than the Anglicized "Jehovah" or even the more Hebrew "Yahweh." Knowing that no matter what name I used wouldn't please everyone, I simply chose to please myself.

Secondly, the narrative device of a "scroll found after the death of the narrator" in a historical novel is not, well, novel. Both Robert Graves (*I, Claudius*) and Mary Renault (*Last of the Wine*) are among the authors who have used it. I tell you this here to give these authors credit for doing this style so much better than I ever could and to recommend to you, the reader, writers I admired greatly who use this method effectively.

I completely invented Ariella and completely invented the idea that she had been Mephibosheth's nurse who crippled him. Let's look at why for a moment. A nurse might possibly have been a young woman, and care for a young royal child would possibly have made her a trusted relative.

A crippled man would not be able to care for a family in the "normal" way of farming/herding/working, and so I created the guilt that the nurse might feel regarding the crippling of such a man. Such guilt might lead her to marry him. Perhaps she, too, had some physically debilitating situation like his because she, in some way, was also undesirable as a mate.

With the possible exception of the Queen of Sheba, no woman in the David/Solomon narrative has more mythology surrounding her than does Bathsheba. While one narrative says her father was Eliam, another text lists her father as Ammiel, which makes it possible that her brother was Machir. There is a Machir listed as one of David's mighty men in one passage. Thus, if Bathsheba was his sister, and this is the same Machir with whom Jonathan's remaining family found refuge in Lo-Debar, it is certainly an interesting coincidence. That would mean it was certainly possible that Bathsheba and Mephibosheth knew each other before their lives crossed again in Jerusalem.

As in any fictional account, other liberties have been taken with the biblical text. Other characters were invented to help move the story along, and some small events also have been created. However, the large events of the lives of David, Mephibosheth, and Solomon come directly from the Bible.

The "kingdom" that David rules isn't, in reality, a kingdom at all. At best, it was a collection of rural tribesmen that collaborated for defensive reasons against vastly superior surrounding enemies. The tribes would follow any leader who promised greater security, so loyalties among them changed regularly as fears increased (or even as they decreased).

In addition, David's Jerusalem was probably nothing more than a hill fortress. It was not a true city in any sense. For dramatic purposes, I have expanded that hill fort into at least a large-sized village. When the Bible lists David's mighty men, you're probably reading the list of virtually all of David's loyal followers/soldiers.

Even Solomon's Jerusalem wasn't much larger, historically. Yet, Solomon's military and constructions projects and large household of dozens of wives and concubines indebted him and Israel heavily. In fact, if the record is correct, Solomon leaves the nation in terrible shape financially, hocked to his ears to people such as King Hiram of Tyre for the building materials of the palace and Temple. As with King David, no historical or archaeological evidence exists of his palace or temple. In fact, with the possible exception of one recently found and fragmentary stone tablet, there is actually no historical record that a Hebrew king named David ever existed. [A fragment of a stone tablet has been discovered that refers to a king in the line of the "House of David", although some scholars debate that interpretation.] The same is true for Solomon.

Solomon's rule in the Bible narrative begins with much bloodshed, although most of the feuds in the story come from David's life. Yet, despite the violent beginning, the text says Solomon is chosen to build God's house because he is not a man of war but rather a man of peace.

Since Israel was a shepherding nation, having a shepherd as its greatest and most beloved king serves as an important symbol for the people as a whole. As with England's King Arthur, the image and the ideal of such a king can often mean more than the actual existence of the individual. In fact, there are many similarities between the mythologies surrounding King David and King Arthur.

So, to say that King David looked out over his "city" and saw Bathsheba on another rooftop "some distance away" is at best a stretch and at worst a complete fabrication. Additionally, David doesn't have to ask who Bathsheba is; he knows her well already. There is no way he could not know her. Interestingly, the Bible narrative has David ask her, "What can I do for you?" when they first "meet."

The Bible also tells of the kings of Judah, after the split between the Twelve Tribes, honoring the mothers of each king. Apparently, the kings kept a chair in the audience room for their mothers; each king of Judah that is listed in the Bible text also lists the mothers of those kings. The story of Israel's history doesn't do this. It is a Davidic tradition. And it appears that Solomon starts that tradition with his own mother, Bathsheba.

And why not? She is the main player in making sure that Solomon secures the throne. In fact, we only have her word as recorded in the biblical text that David has promised the throne to Solomon at all. David only agrees with her, but perhaps in his aged and sick condition he is easily suggestible.

Finally, *Psalm 23*—a chapter perhaps more beloved than any other in the Bible—is not said to have been written by David for anyone in particular. Perhaps David, as a shepherd, sees the analogy of God-as-shepherd as too plain to ignore for his own life, and he simply wrote it for himself.

However, taking the meaning of Lo-Debar to be "no pasture," and seeing the drastic change in the life and fortune of Mephibosheth when David brought him to Jerusalem, the connection is impossible to ignore. The change in life meant so much to him and his little family; the move from the insecurity of Lo-Debar to the security of David's table makes *Psalm 23* apply directly to the young man's life.

And it applies to all our lives when we think of our change in status from "dogs" to desired, from that of alienation from God to that of beloved children, from our own, self-imposed Lo-Debars to His amazing pastures of tender grass.

ABOUT THE AUTHOR

Charles Millson is a lifelong south-erner. He is a teacher, minister, and advocate in a small town in middle Tennessee. After teaching in the Memphis, Tennessee area for over a decade, Millson turned his attention and talents to ministry in Romania and Costa Rica. He is also the author of *More Than Rubies, a Bible* workbook that looks at the lessons we can learn from the lives of some of the lesser-known women of the Hebrew Scriptures. He has also published a book of poetry, has been published in *The Old Hickory Review*, and has been a contributor to *People's World*. His sports writing has been featured on such blogs as Rivals.com, where he was a managing editor, and on *Bleacher Report*. His ministry has taken him to work in the inner-city with low income housing, and currently he heads a nonprofit food bank in his small town. He can be heard weekly on a one hour radio talk-show called Westmoreland Wednes-days on WTNK out of Hartsville, Tennessee. In addi-tion, Millson is a minister at a church in Westmoreland, Tennessee. He is the father of one son, Shawn, and he enjoys spending time with his English bulldog, Bucky.

Faith is the assurance of things hoped for. It is the conviction of things not seen.

FAITH FOR A
DARK SATURDAY
James T. Baker

"The darkest hour is just before the dawn"—this age-old adage has been born out over countless lives as a true statement. In *Faith for a Dark Saturday*, the noted theologian and historian James Baker shows how nine men from the Bible prove the point. Each man tells, in his own words, the misery of his darkest hour, a time that he did not know but we do was just before the dawning of a morning of hope. Abraham as he prepared to sacrifice his only son Isaac; Jacob as he prepared to meet his hostile brother and possible death; Moses in desert exile before he sees the burning bush and receives the commission of his life; King Hezekiah as he awaits assault from the invincible Assyrian army; Joseph as he contemplates the scandal caused by his finance's pregnancy, the apostle Peter on the Saturday between the crucifixion and resurrection; Paul as he prepares to leave for Damascus to round up Christians; the jailer of Philippi before the earthquake that will bring his salvation; and John in exile on Patmos before his vision. You will be inspired to lean on your own faith as you share the experiences of these men, caught in fear and despair, during the agony of their own dark Saturdays, just before the dawn of a new day of hope.